MW00882142

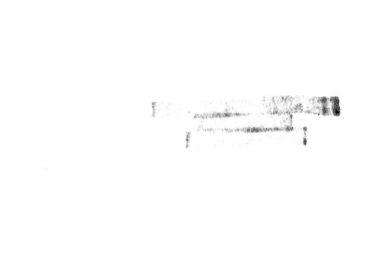

TEXAS FRIDAYS

AUSTIN

SAM MOUSSAVI

EPIC
Press

Austin
Texas Fridays

Written by Sam Moussavi

Copyright © 2017 by Abdo Consulting Group, Inc.

Published by EPIC Press™
PO Box 398166
Minneapolis, MN 55439

Printed in the United States of America.

Cover design by Kali Yeado
Images for cover art obtained from iStockPhoto.com
Edited by Gil Conrad

LIBRARY OF CONGRESS CATALOGING-IN-PUBLICATION DATA

Names: Moussavi, Sam, author.
Title: Austin / by Sam Moussavi.
Description: Minneapolis, MN : EPIC Press, 2017. | Series: Texas Fridays
Summary: Stevie McCrae was born and raised in Austin, and it has always been his dream to
   play running back at University of Texas-Austin. If it were up to him, he wouldn't leave his
   beloved hometown until the NFL came calling. Problem is, Stevie never gets any recruiting
   love from UT. Can Stevie lead his team to a state championship, and prove he's got what it
   takes?
Identifiers: LCCN 2016946186 | ISBN 9781680764918 (lib. bdg.)
   | ISBN 9781680765472 (ebook)
Subjects: LCSH: High school—Fiction. | Football—Fiction. | Football players—Fiction. | Life
   change events—Fiction. | Young adult fiction.
Classification: DDC [Fic]—dc23
LC record available at http://lccn.loc.gov/2016946186

EPIC
Press

EPICPRESS.COM

For those eager to take liberties with the imagination and stay awhile.

—Pete Simonelli

1

"**YO, WHERE THESE GIRLS AT?**" JERON ASKED.

"I don't know," Stevie responded, a little annoyed at his rock-headed friend. "You're the one who set it up."

Stevie McCrae and Jeron Peters were teammates on the Stephen F. Austin High School varsity football team. They were both seniors. They had each been an important part of the team as juniors the season before. On the field, there was one major difference between the friends: size. Jeron *looked* like a football player at six foot three and two hundred pounds. He was the Austin Maroons' starting and had two athletic scholarship offers from Texas schools, Texas A&M and the University of Texas–Austin. Stevie did not look like a football player at first glance. Sure, he was squat and muscular, but his height—barely five-foot-six—didn't convey the image of gridiron greatness in anyone's mind.

The two friends' size disparity rendered the sight of them standing next to each other downright comical. Stevie looked more the part of little brother rather than football equal. But size difference aside, the two were best friends. As they waited outside the movie theater for their double dates to arrive, Stevie couldn't keep himself from asking Jeron an important question.

"You taking the offer from UT?"

Jeron smiled because he knew it would burn Stevie. No malice intended, just a little fun.

"I don't know yet," Jeron said. "It's down to UT and A&M."

Stevie shook his head.

"You don't need to be worrying about all that

"You don't need to be worrying about all that right now," Jeron said, moving on to more important business. "Just worry about these two girls showing up. You know the rule: don't believe when a white girl says that she is going to come out with you. You got to *see* it."

"I don't care about these girls," Stevie said with a dismissive hand wave. "I'm only doing this for you. As a favor."

"I'm the one doing you a favor. You might get some ass out of this."

"Whatever, man."

"Besides," Jeron said with another smile, "you shouldn't be worried about me going to UT."

"Why?"

"'Cause you ain't gonna be joining me there with your midget ass."

Jeron started laughing, and Stevie's ferocity kicked in. He got low, clamped Jeron's legs, and lifted him into the air. Jeron couldn't stop laughing.

Stevie dumped his friend onto the sidewalk and stood over him with a balled up right fist in the air.

"I'm just playin', man," Jeron said, still laughing. "Just playin'!"

"Hi there, boys," a throaty voice said from behind them.

Jeron looked up and Stevie turned around. The two girls had arrived.

"What are you studs doing?" the same voice asked. "Playing grab ass?"

Jeron picked himself up off the sidewalk, dusted off his hands, and eyed the two girls like candy.

"Nah," he said. "Just waiting on you."

The one who spoke first was Natasha Diamante, and her friend was Madison Wilks. Natasha was blonde, with a bubble butt and an infatuation for football players, especially if they were talented and black. She had a defined reputation inside the halls of Stephen F. Austin High. The other one, Madison, was plainer looking, but cute in her own right. Stevie noticed right away that Madison did not want to be there. He couldn't say what it was that told him this. It was a feeling he had. Stevie thought that, like him, Madison was simply doing a favor for a friend.

Natasha put a hand on her hip and waited for Jeron to come over—as *he* was the one she wanted, the big, strapping one. She and Madison hadn't discussed beforehand who would go with whom. Natasha just took what she wanted.

Ever the equal opportunist, Jeron didn't really care which one he *got*. As long as the girl was down, he wasn't picky.

"Should we get tickets to the show?" Jeron asked.

"Yeah," Natasha said, coming forward and taking Jeron by the arm. They walked into the theater, leaving Madison and Stevie behind.

The movie was one of those action duds that lost everyone's interest fifteen minutes in. The premise of this one had to do with an action hero relegated to the use of a wheel chair. Jeron and Natasha began sucking face during the coming attractions, so the plot of the film couldn't have mattered to them any less. Stevie, on the other hand, gave the movie a shot, and the same could be said for Madison. They both chuckled at the ridiculousness toward the beginning where the bi-wheeled protagonist dispatched two heavily bearded, vaguely olive-skinned men, with only a handsaw. The interest was short lived, however. Stevie and Madison yawned when the blonde, supermodel clone of a love interest was wedged into the story shortly after the testosterone-filled opening.

When all hope was lost with regard to the film, Stevie looked over and saw Jeron and Natasha still engaged. He then looked at Madison.

"Is she always like that?" he asked.

"Is he?" Madison replied.

"I guess they're perfect for each other."

"I know."

"You don't have to go along with what's happening over there," Stevie said with a nod down the aisle. "I didn't come out tonight to get laid."

"What's the matter? You don't like me?" Madison asked, feigning insecurity.

"No I didn't say that," he said. "It's just that I don't know you."

"Who said that *I* wanted to make out with you?"

"Okay, okay," he said. "You're right. I jumped the gun. But it is kind of weird to just start making out with someone without saying a word, right?"

"I've never heard a football player talk like this before."

Now it was Stevie's turn to lay it on thick. He backed away from Madison and gave her the crook eye.

"How many football players have you been around in a situation like this?"

Madison smiled. She jabbed a thumb in the direction of Jeron and Natasha.

"Well Natasha loves football players. And she's my friend. So . . . "

Stevie waited for the rest of it because he was engaged now.

Seeing his intent on listening, Madison couldn't help but toy with his assumptions. "But you want to know if I've ever been the one with my tongue down one of your teammates' throats, don't you?"

Stevie gulped. He'd never heard a girl speak this way.

"The answer is *no.*"

They locked eyes, and Madison giggled because that's what she always did when she looked into the eyes of someone she liked. With the situation diffused, Stevie laughed as well.

"Tell me something about yourself," he said.

Madison lifted her head as she thought; and right then in that moment, Stevie thought she was beautiful.

"Well, I like to cook," Madison said.

Her excitement on the matter was conveyed through her eyes. As a running back, Stevie had become adept at reading people's eyes. On the football field, with every defender larger than him,

Stevie's gift of perception saved him from getting killed out there.

"I mean *really* cook," Madison said. "Not just hamburgers and salads and things like that. My goal is to become chef of my own restaurant."

"Cool."

A couple sitting in the row ahead turned in unison and glared at Stevie and Madison.

"Shh!" the couple huffed, again in unison.

"Sorry," Madison whispered to the couple.

"What about you?" Madison whispered, leaning in close. "Tell me something about yourself that's not about football."

Stevie thought, and it didn't take long to realize that football *was* his life. Something clicked and he snapped his fingers.

"Okay," he whispered. "This is kind of related to football but not all the way."

"What is it?"

"I hate how short I am. If there were one thing

I could change about myself, I would make myself taller."

"You mean you wouldn't declare world peace or end hunger?"

"Hell no."

"That's terrible," Madison said with a muted, belly laugh.

"I would give myself like, four, maybe five extra inches. Just talking about it right now makes me angry."

"Why?"

"It's caused so many problems for me, on and off the field," he continued. "I grew up fighting just to get respect. And now, colleges aren't taking me seriously."

"It's okay," Madison whispered because she thought that's what Stevie wanted to hear.

Stevie shook his head, but his eyes softened. He liked this girl.

. . . .

After the movie, the foursome headed over to one of those "farm to table" restaurants that were sprouting up all over Austin. The restaurant was next to UT's campus, and that irked Stevie. He loved the University of Texas, but the emotion was not reciprocated. Stevie was not a realistic option for a school that historically favored big running backs like Earl Campbell and Ricky Williams.

"What's the matter?" Madison asked, leaning in close.

"Nothing," Stevie said, exiting his introspection. "I'm cool."

Jeron and Natasha were across from Stevie and Madison at an elevated four top. It was nice to see Jeron and Natasha without their faces glued together.

"So," Natasha said. "You guys gonna win state this year?"

Jeron pointed to his teammate. "It depends on what he and his boys on offense do. I got the 'D' on lock."

"Oh yeah," Stevie said. "That's why last year in the first round of the playoffs y'all got shredded. We put up forty-five and the defense—his defense—gave up forty-eight."

That painful loss in the bi-district round of the playoffs left a bitter taste in every single mouth that cared about Austin football. The loss was scarring for members of Austin's defense. Jeron still suffered the occasional nightmare from dropping a key interception that would've sealed the win for the Maroons. Stevie had an easier time letting go because he ran for two hundred yards and four touchdowns in the playoff game.

"Easy, boys," Natasha said. "What are we gonna order?"

The four of them looked at the menus.

"I just want some wings," Jeron said. "They got wings?"

Madison chuckled.

"What?" Jeron asked.

"Why don't we let our future chef here tell us what's good?" Natasha said, with a nod to Madison.

Madison didn't say anything right away.

"Well?" Natasha said with a look over to her friend.

"Uh-uh," Jeron said. "I want some wings."

"They don't have wings here, dumbass," Stevie said. "Can you read?"

He and Madison cracked up as Jeron's eyes became daggers. Natasha joined in the laughter as well.

"I don't know why y'all brought me over to this place with this whack-ass menu. Could've just gone to PJ's," Jeron said.

"I'll order for the table," Madison said. "You'll like it."

. . . .

Madison ordered six dishes for the table to share, and everyone enjoyed the picks, even Jeron. When the waiter brought the dishes, Madison explained what was in each one and how it was prepared. The only one who paid any attention to this was Stevie. He could see how much food meant to Madison, and he appreciated her passion.

Natasha was able to "charm" the bartender into selling the underage foursome a couple rounds of beers. She and Jeron had two each while Stevie had one. Madison drank water only. When they finished up with their dinner and drinks, they split the bill four ways. Natasha went over to thank the bartender, and when she did so, the goateed UT student asked for her number. She jotted it down on a napkin and slid it across the bar.

"What was that?" Jeron asked as Natasha joined the others outside. "You gave him your digits?"

"No, baby," Natasha said. "I mean, yeah, I gave him my number, but I was just being polite."

"Don't be giving out your number when you're with me," he said.

Stevie chuckled.

"I'm sorry, baby," Natasha said before kissing him on the lips. And they started going at it again right in front of the restaurant.

2

NATASHA'S PARENTS LIVED FIFTEEN MINUTES EAST of UT's campus. When the foursome pulled up, it was pretty clear that the Diamantes were football fans. Stevie's eyes were drawn to a garage door painted burnt orange, the staple color of the University of Texas.

When they walked inside, Natasha flicked on some lights that revealed an even deeper obsession with the Texas Longhorns. The living room's shag carpet was also burnt orange, and even the throw pillows were shaped like little footballs with "Hook 'Em Horns" stitched into the fabric. The walls were covered with memorabilia, ranging from old team portraits to signed jerseys.

"My folks love the Horns," Natasha said lamely.

"Stevie loves 'em too," Jeron said with a smirk.

"Let me get us some liquor," Natasha said.

"I'm just gonna have one more beer," Stevie said.

"Okay, be right back," she said.

Natasha left the three of them in the living room. From another room, rap music began to thump.

Madison sat down on the couch first, and Stevie and Jeron followed. Natasha reentered with a few beers, a bottle of whisky, and two glasses. She set everything on the coffee table and handed a beer to Stevie. She poured herself and Jeron a half-glass of whisky each and then raised her glass.

"This is to y'all having an amazing season and winning State," she said.

The three drinkers touched glass before taking their first sips, only Natasha's wasn't a sip—she drank down her whisky in one shot. Her face flushed and eyes narrowed to predatory slits.

"Now you," she said to Jeron. "You come with me."

Jeron stood up with his glass. Natasha grabbed the whisky bottle.

Stevie raised his beer to the couple as they went upstairs, leaving him and Madison alone.

Stevie leaned forward and looked around the living room.

"Does she have siblings?"

"Christ, no," Madison said. "Natasha's enough of a handful for her folks."

"I see her hittin' that liquor pretty hard," he said. "My dad says when you see a person doing that, there's something to it."

"He's right."

The two of them sat silently in the living room. The sound of the music covered up whatever was happening upstairs. Both Stevie and Madison were glad for that.

"What about you? Any siblings?" Madison asked.

"I have an older brother and a younger sister."

"Did your brother play football?"

"He played a little college ball. Nothing past that. He's always harping on me to focus on my education. I get it, but I want to make football my career. You?"

"I have an older sister," Madison said. "She goes to, of course, UT. Sorry, I can tell you have a thing with UT, but it's right here. You can't avoid it living in Austin."

"I know," he said. "But it's pretty crazy in *here,* right?"

"Yes. It's bizarre," she said.

They laughed together again. Stevie couldn't remember the last time he had laughed this much with a girl. After it subsided, they sat silently once again. But it wasn't uncomfortable for either of them. Stevie placed his beer down on a UT coaster.

"So."

"So?"

"You know what?" Stevie asked.

"What?" Madison replied.

"I like you. There's something about you that I like."

"Just one thing?"

"No, I didn't mean it like that."

"I'm just kidding," she said with a smile.

"I don't meet many girls like you."

"What? You mean the girls at the football parties?"

"Yeah, girls like," he said, "well, girls like Natasha."

Madison smiled.

"You're nothing like Natasha. What are you even doing hanging out with her?"

"We're very different. That's true. But Natasha and I have been friends for a long time. She's had my back on some things. I don't always agree with her choices. But she is a friend."

"Fair enough."

And then there was a silence all through the house. The music had stopped and luckily for Stevie and Madison, there weren't any other noises coming from upstairs.

"I could say the same about you," Madison said.

"About?"

"About you and Jeron."

"It's funny. I haven't really thought about that until I saw you and Natasha tonight. I guess me and Jeron are the same. We both play ball."

"Well," Madison said, "do you want to make out with me now?"

"Whoa! Where did that come from? We're getting all deep and you hit me with the make-out proposition."

"Just making sure of one way you're different from Jeron," Madison said.

"I'll do you one better though," Stevie said. "I want you to be my girlfriend."

Madison smiled and her face flushed. "Am I blushing?"

Stevie smiled. "I don't know, but you look good."

"You really want me to be your girl? Just like that?"

"Yeah," Stevie said, "Just like that."

"Why would you want to be with me?" Madison asked. "There are much prettier girls at school."

"I think you are prettier than all of them."

She blushed again.

"Well, do you like me?" he asked.

"Yes."

"Then we're together."

Stevie leaned in and they kissed. "I have to ask you one thing," he said, pulling away from her. "Will your parents have a problem because I'm black?"

"No. They're not like that."

"Cool."

3

STEVIE WOKE UP EXCITED THE NEXT MORNING, NOT only because he had a new girlfriend, but also Austin High's number one offense would go up against its number one defense later that afternoon at practice. There would be a scout from UT there, with an eye on Jeron and few other Austin players. The practice would be Stevie's chance to make another impression on a school that, up to that point, had rejected him fully. Despite setting state rushing records as a junior, the University of Texas would not even give Stevie a look. When Austin High's head coach, Bill Moffit, had put in a call to UT on

Stevie's behalf, they essentially said, "Thanks, but no thanks."

Undaunted, Stevie put together a highlight tape of his best plays from junior year and sent it to UT, but the school was left unimpressed. UT wasn't the only school that had an issue with his size. The scholarship offers Stevie received were from either Division–II colleges in Texas or junior colleges around the southwest. He had not accepted any of those standing offers, holding out hope that one more year of record-breaking stats would change the minds of UT scouts.

· ·

As Austin High's starting tailback, there were no questions regarding Stevie's role within the team. He *was* the team, at least on offense. Austin High's coaches loved to run the ball, and that strength often came at the expense of the passing game. During Stevie's first two years on varsity, Austin's passing attack could be politely referred to as "developmental." But a one-sided team doesn't go far in Texas. Although Stevie's ability was enough to carry the team into the Six A District Two Playoffs at the end of both of his varsity seasons, he was too beat up to carry the team any further. And without even the threat of a viable passing game, first-round playoff exits became Austin High's reality.

This season—Stevie's senior year—would be different. Coach Moffit had finally found a legitimate quarterback during the offseason: Johnny Muretti.

"What's up, Stevie?" Muretti asked, as the offense took a water break at practice.

Muretti was named an offensive captain, joining Stevie as the only other captain on that side of the ball.

"Hey, man."

"I'm gonna loosen it up for you this season, I promise."

"I believe you," Stevie said, because he really had no other choice.

Stevie had heard it all before—that *this* quarterback

would be the one to finally unlock the true potential of Austin's offense—but decided to keep his doubts to himself. Besides, he didn't have time to worry about anyone else. The University of Texas didn't care that Stevie never played with a real quarterback. It was Coach Moffit's job to fix the weakness, and it was Stevie's job to continue playing at the standard he set, no matter how high it was.

The two offensive captains shook hands, and Stevie went back to his pre-practice stretches. He had invited Madison to practice, but she had a shift at the restaurant where she worked. Stevie's eyes wandered into the stands and focused on a group in the first row. They were scouts—every player knew their faces. There was the droopy-eyed one from Tech, the pudgy-faced one from Baylor, and of course, the goateed one from UT.

"You're gonna see this year," Stevie muttered as he eyed UT's scout.

Jeron came up from behind and popped Stevie in the shoulder pad.

"What up, negro?"

Stevie nodded and the two shook.

"Natasha wanted to go all night," he said. "Wearin' a brother out."

"Well I hope you saved some energy because I'm coming straight at you."

"You don't want none of this," Jeron replied, flexing his right bicep.

The whistle blew and Moffit called up the team in a circle at midfield.

"Okay guys," Coach Moffit said, "we're gonna treat this like a real game. We're keeping score, going full speed. Two rules. No hits around the knees or head and do not—I repeat, do not—hit the quarterbacks."

There was a slight groan from the defensive players.

Stevie shook his head. *Dumbasses*, he thought.

"I want the number ones on both sides to stay out on the field," Coach Moffit said, breaking the circle.

Johnny Muretti entered the huddle and called out the first play: an off-tackle power run to the right. This play was Stevie's favorite—a bread and butter staple of Austin's offense that worked mainly because of the chemistry between Stevie and the right side of his offensive line. The right guard, Colt Mackey, and right tackle, Ty Worrington, were seniors like Stevie and had been starting on varsity since they were soph-omores. What made this play a repeated success was Stevie's ability to feel out the exact moment when he needed either to cut it inside or bounce it outside, based on the work of his linemen on the right side. Mackey and Worrington knew they simply had to give Stevie a crease to take it all the way.

When the ball was snapped, Stevie exploded toward the line of scrimmage. Muretti extended the ball out, and Stevie met him with his arms open. With the ball lodged into his gut, Stevie could now focus on how the play was developing. When he saw that the defensive tackle had shot the gap on Mackey, he bounced it outside. Stevie dodged one would-be tackler in the backfield, and from there, it was a race to the edge.

Near the sideline, there was a collision waiting

to happen with Jeron pursuing from his middle linebacker spot. When the moment of truth came, Stevie put his foot in the ground and made a sharp cut back inside, leaving Jeron to whiff on his tackle attempt. It was a foot race now, and the result of the play was an eighty-yard touchdown run.

The starting members of Austin's offense sprinted down to the end zone to celebrate with Stevie. The few who didn't join them stayed busy trash-talking the defense. On his way back to the huddle, Stevie shot a glance to the scout from UT. The scout remained stone-faced.

Muretti shared the next play, a pass that called for all eligible receivers on the field to run "go" routes, straight down the field. Stevie's job was to stay in the backfield and help with pass protection. It was Muretti's job to hang in the pocket, find the receiver that wins on his route, and let it fly.

Before the snap, Stevie anticipated that the defense was coming with a blitz. He knew from experience that Jeron liked to blitz up the middle. Stevie's eyes followed Jeron pre-snap, searching for any indicator in the linebacker's body language that would tip off a blitz. But there wasn't any such signal. Jeron was good in his own right and seasoned too—one of the best defenders Stevie had ever faced. If Jeron were coming on a blitz, it would be disguised until the last possible moment.

On the snap, Jeron shot right through the left guard and center. He made a straight line for Muretti. Right before making the sack, Stevie clobbered Jeron on a blitz pickup. There was the collective drone of "ooh!" from the sideline. Muretti stepped up into the pocket and launched a pass to Austin's junior receiver, Hank Auckland, streaking down the left side. The pass hit Auckland in stride, and the receiver walked in for the touchdown.

That made two plays for two eighty-yard touchdowns. And on both plays, Stevie was the principal reason for success. His versatility was startling. As if he hadn't done enough for the team in the past, his blitz pickup was now a weapon for the offense.

With Stevie finding new ways to elevate his game, coupled with Muretti's emergence, perhaps Austin High's offense could finally reach its fullest potential?

Stevie helped Jeron off the turf. The stud middle linebacker was still groggy from the hit laid upon him by the "too-small to play big-time college football" running back.

"Go to sleep, boy," Stevie said, with a smile and pat to Jeron's behind.

Jeron found no humor in the remark and really didn't appreciate getting embarrassed in front of the scouts and all his teammates.

"Man, you need to chill out," Jeron said.

"What?"

"Scouts are up there in the stands"

"So?" Stevie shot back. "You make me better. I make you better. Remember that?"

"You can't be making me look weak out here, Stevie," Jeron pleaded. "I got it all on the line."

"Like I don't?" Stevie replied.

Stevie continued as a one-man wrecking crew during the balance of practice. He finished with seven carries for two hundred yards and three touchdowns against Austin's number one defense. He was also productive in the passing game, catching two passes for fifty yards and picking up three more blitzes with the same fury and force as the one on Jeron.

Muretti had acquitted himself well too. He went eight for eight with one hundred sixty yards and three touchdowns. All this occurred against Austin's first-string defense, and Stevie was excited. Finally, the prospect of steady quarterback play. Coach Moffit was thrilled by the development, though as head coach, he was responsible for worrying about the entire team, not just the offense. In his instant-analysis, the downside of the first string offense's utter domination was that the defense, thought to be the stronger of the two units, was now a question mark. His dream—and any head coach's dream—was a squad that exhibited balance.

Jeron didn't play up to his standard and was clearly a different player. Jeron and Stevie had no other direct exchanges during the time that the first strings were competing. Stevie knew the block stung his friend's ego and made his way off the practice field without further comment.

Before hitting the locker room, Stevie decided to reintroduce himself to UT's scout, who was now on the field talking with one of his teammates. Stevie felt that his play during practice must have made an impression on the scout. There was just no way the scout could overlook that sort of production.

The teammate whom the scout was talking with was a sophomore named Lance Monroe. Monroe was a six-foot-five defensive end with barely any muscle on his frame. During practice, Stevie had made Monroe look foolish and felt a burn in his gut when overhearing that the UT scout was more interested in Monroe's potential rather than in what Stevie brought to the table *right now.*

The scout saw Stevie out of the corner of his eye and excused himself from Monroe. Stevie buried the negative thoughts and approached with an open right hand.

"Hello, sir," Stevie said. "We've met before, but I just wanted to say hello again. My name is Stevie McCrae." He shot a firm hand into the scout's and shook with force and purpose—something his father taught him.

"Nice job out there today, Stevie," the scout said. "You're a fine player."

"Thank you, sir," Stevie said. "I just want you to know that I'd do anything to wear the burnt orange. If you need any information on me, just ask my coach."

The scout winced before smiling uneasily. "Thank you, Stevie," he said. "We have everything we need right now."

Stevie nodded and remained frozen. The scout

turned his back and rejoined his conversation with Monroe. Stevie witnessed the scout's enthusiasm as he talked with Monroe, who up to that point had not proved himself at the varsity level.

* * *

After a shower and change of clothes, Stevie knocked on Moffit's half-opened door.

"Coach, can I talk to you for a second?"

Coach Moffit was at his desk. He looked up to Stevie and took off his reading glasses. "Sure, Stevie."

Stevie entered and took a seat across from his coach.

"What's up?"

"I saw the scout from UT on the field after practice talking to Lance. Are they looking at him already? He hasn't even played a down on varsity."

"Yeah. They like his size. These big schools love size and they love potential. You know that, Stevie."

"Yeah. I was just hoping . . . " Stevie took a deep breath.

"What's wrong?" Coach Moffit asked.

"I was hoping you could put in another call to UT. I mean, I'll produce like that every game this season," Stevie said, jabbing a finger toward where the practice field would be. "They can't deny that. I mean, it doesn't, or at least it shouldn't, matter how short I am. It's about what I can do *on* the field."

"I've talked to them about you during both seasons you've been up here. You know how I feel about you. But UT—at least right now—they're just not interested."

"There's nothing else you can do?"

"I'm sorry. No matter how many times I tell them about your value to our program, they aren't ready to offer you a scholarship. Your size is a non-starter. For the record, I think they are dead wrong about you. I think you would be an asset to UT."

Stevie stood up, but his coach hadn't finished with his suggestion.

"I'm getting a lot of calls on you from smaller schools though. Don't get caught up in the size of the school. You have chances to play college ball."

"I'll see you tomorrow, Coach."

Moffit stood up and patted his star running back on the shoulder. "*I* know how much you mean to us."

"Thanks Coach, but that doesn't matter when it comes to UT. *They* need to see it." He left the office.

Jeron was waiting by Stevie's car in the parking lot. He nodded when Stevie approached, and Stevie nodded back.

"What's up?" Jeron asked.

"Nothing much."

"You see the UT scout talking to Lance?"

"Yeah I saw."

"That scout should be talking to you. No one on the field can touch you."

"Yeah, well, it doesn't matter what you, me, or Coach Moffit thinks. It's all just talk."

Jeron shifted his stance. "My bad about that stuff with the block. I didn't mean to come at you like that. You was right. We all go hard when we're between those lines. What I said was wrong."

"It's all good."

"Cool. Now, can you hook a brother up with a ride?"

"Yeah, get in."

After the two friends got into the car, Stevie started it up and pulled out of the school's parking lot.

"I heard you and Madison are together."

"Heard?"

"From Natasha."

Stevie nodded. "What about you and Natasha?"

"What about us?" Jeron said with incredulity.

Stevie smiled.

"I'm not really a one-girl type," Jeron said.

Stevie shrugged.

"You gonna go see her right now?" Jeron asked.

Stevie smiled for the first time since practice ended. "Yeah. I'm gonna pick her up from work."

4

AFTER DROPPING JERON OFF, STEVIE DROVE TO A restaurant near the UT campus called *The Dutch Oven*. Madison was standing out front, holding a to-go box. When she saw Stevie's car, her face lit up. She hopped into the passenger seat.

"Hi," she said. "How did it go?"

"It went good. How was your day?"

"Busy," she said. "I brought you dinner."

"You didn't have to," he said. "I was thinking we'd grab a burger or something."

"I can't look at food right now."

"Okay."

"It's a salad, and the grill man threw in a little piece of steak."

"That sounds awesome. Thanks."

"The chef is a really good guy. He told me if I keep working hard, I'll move up fast."

"That steak does *smell* good," Stevie said. "I know a place that's quiet we could go to. Is that cool?"

"Sure."

Stevie drove to the secluded spot he had frequented since he was a boy. It was a wide field of grass next to old railroad tracks. There was also a picnic table next to the now defunct terminal.

He parked and they walked over to the table. Madison placed the to-go box in front of him before rooting inside her purse for a set of silverware she had borrowed from the restaurant. The set was wrapped in a napkin.

"I gotta take these back tomorrow," she said.

Stevie opened the box. A crisp green salad with red beets and a hunk of charred meat stared back at him.

"Mmm," he said, taking a whiff.

"The dressing is on the side," she said. "It's a ginger dressing—my recipe. I wasn't sure if you'd like it, so I played it safe."

"If you made it," he said, "I know it's good."

"What is this place?"

"Oh, I been coming here for a while," Stevie said. "Sometimes I need a nice, quiet place to think. And this place does it for me."

Madison watched Stevie as he popped the lid off the dressing container and poured some over the salad. He went in for a bite of meat first and it melted in his mouth.

"Wow," he said.

He took a bite of the dressed salad next and it was just as delicious.

"You made all this?"

"Not the meat," she said. "For now, I prepare the salads, dressings and sauces. You like the dressing?"

"Like it?" he said, before taking another bite. "It's one of the best things I've ever tasted.

"I'm glad."

"I'm glad we didn't go for that burger."

"Tell me more about the scrimmage."

"There's not much to tell," he said, in between another bite of steak. "Business as usual for me."

"So why do you seem upset when we talk about it?"

"Do I?"

Madison nodded. Stevie leaned the silverware on the to-go box and wiped his mouth.

"I saw the scout from UT, you know, after practice. And he was talking to another guy on the team who hasn't played a game on the varsity level yet. He just has the size UT is looking for."

"So you're upset because they're looking past you?"

Stevie looked past Madison and into the field before meeting her eyes. "More like right through me—like no matter what I *do* they can't see me. I always wanted to play for UT. It's my dream."

"I'm sure there are a lot of other schools that would want a player like you."

"I know that," Stevie said. "It's just to play college ball in the place I grew up—my family and friends are here and could always be at the games. I don't know, but I just haven't pictured it any other way."

"I say, forget about them then. If they can't see you, maybe they don't deserve you."

"You're sweet, but for me, it doesn't work that way. When somebody tells me I can't do something, I can't help trying to prove them wrong. It's like, the more they ignore me, the more driven I become. Hell, people thought I was too small to play varsity ball, and I've rewritten the state history books."

"I get that. I mean, I know what it's like to want to prove people wrong," she said. "I'm just saying that it's not worth stressing over something you can't change."

"I can change it."

"How?"

"I have to be even better this season than in the

past. That means more yards and more touchdowns. *And* I have to lead the team to a state championship. That's the one thing missing from my resumé. We've never won a playoff game in my time at Austin High."

Madison nodded her head. Stevie had convinced her of his intentions solely on strength of his passion.

"Do you think you guys can really win a championship?"

Stevie slapped his right thigh.

"I think I got enough magic in these legs," he said. "I'm not trying to sound cocky or anything, but I do think it's possible. I think I'm good enough."

To Madison, this wasn't the same testosterone-laden bravado she had witnessed from other football jocks at Austin High. There was something genuine about Stevie. Something pure. She wouldn't go so far as to call Stevie's dream "naïve." It was just that his intentions weren't steeped in some urge to exclaim superiority over the other students at Austin High. Stevie was way beyond that. He had his sights aimed on something much more meaningful. His wish was to push his talent as far as it could go. Just like her. Madison could dig that.

"Okay," she said. "I'm behind you."

She leaned in and gave Stevie a kiss.

"Now let me ask *you* something," Stevie said, putting his arm around Madison and pulling her in close. "What's the deal with you and food? I can see that you love it and that you got skills. What's your plan?"

"I don't know," she said. "It's like you and football, I guess. It comes natural to me. When I wake up in the morning, instead of thinking about school, I think of flavor combinations. Being in the kitchen gives me a feeling that I don't get anywhere else."

"Yeah. I feel you on that. That's how I feel when I'm out on the field."

"I want to be an executive chef one day."

"What's that?"

"The executive chef of a restaurant is the one in

charge of coming up with the menu. Right now, I'm preparing food on someone else's menu. I'm not the one coming up with the ideas."

"Well, I believe in you," Stevie said, with a smile. "I know you'll be an executive chef one day."

They got back into the car and didn't talk on the ride to Madison's house. Madison did, however, reach over and hold Stevie's hand. While she squeezed it, Stevie thought about the other girls he'd been involved with other the years. None of them evoked the feeling that Madison had in Stevie's heart. None of them seemed to care like she did. And most importantly, he had never cared about a girl like he did for Madison. They had just met, but it felt like they had known each other for a long while.

"This is it," she said.

Stevie parked in front of her house.

Madison leaned over and put her arms around Stevie. They kissed a few times and she lingered before getting out of the car. Before walking through the door, she turned back to wave. He waved back and waited for her to get inside before heading home.

5

"WHAT'S UP, CHAMP?" A VOICE ASKED FROM overhead.

Stevie was half-asleep in bed. His father had always called him "champ" growing up, and it stuck, even though he had never won a championship on any level. He opened his eyes with a grin. The smell of bacon and coffee were coming on strong from downstairs. Sundays were special at the McCrae house—a day of relaxation and reconnection. Every person in the house was busy with either work or sports during the week, so the last day of the week always provided a much needed, albeit brief, respite for family, food, and laughs.

"I'm sorry I missed practice yesterday," Stevie's father, Wilton said. "There was a problem at the dealership. The lighting in the showroom went haywire. All my best cars were in the dark."

"It's cool, Dad."

"How'd it go?"

"I was a beast out there. After the scrimmage, I saw the scout from UT," Stevie said before he shook his head. "No love."

"Alright, son," Wilton said. "Get washed up and come downstairs. Your mother cooked breakfast, and your brother will be here any minute."

"Okay."

Wilton McCrae Jr. was a bit of an Austin football legend in his own right. After starring at defensive back at Austin High, Wilton went on to play four years of college ball at Louisiana Tech University. He wasn't good enough to make it to the NFL, but he did receive four years of quality college education and a BA in Business Administration. After graduating from LA Tech, he returned to his home state of Texas, parlaying his natural business acumen into part ownership of the most successful car dealership in Austin.

He now owned that same dealership outright and planned on leaving it to his kids. Wilton loved all of his three kids equally. But it was his bond with Stevie that felt the strongest. Stevie's older brother, Jackson or "Jack," as the family called him, was a good player at Austin High as well. Though not as talented a player as Stevie or Wilton, Jack walked on to play college ball at tiny LaGrange College, a Division III school in Georgia.

Wilton nurtured Stevie's love for the game of football, just like he did with Jack and Stevie's thirteen-year-old sister, Naomi, a budding sprinter. Stevie was the child who responded most to Wilton's attention. To make it clear, Wilton was not one of those fathers who expected his kids to be athletes simply because he was an athlete. He would love and support his kids no matter what they chose to do. But sports *were* in their blood. Stevie also inherited Wilton's trait of refusing to be denied when underestimated, strengthening their bond further. Wilton and Stevie hated to be viewed as the underdogs and this fact was never lost on Wilton. He saw himself in Stevie, and knew his middle child had what it took to go far in the game of football. Maybe further than any McCrae had ever gone.

. . . .

Stevie washed up, went downstairs and joined Naomi, Wilton and his mother, Ebony, in the kitchen. Besides a full spread of eggs, bacon, toast, fruit salad, orange juice, and coffee on the kitchen table, there were three choices of cereal as well. Wilton sat in his usual seat at the family's circular breakfast table. He sipped his coffee and read the morning edition of *The Statesman* with intent written all over his face. Ebony put the finishing touches on her coffee, and Naomi was at the refrigerator fetching the milk.

He went over and gave his mother a kiss, and she touched his face like always. She let her hand linger because these chances were few and far between with his busy schedule.

"That's turkey bacon, in case you're wondering," she said. "I know you're in-season."

The front door opened and Jack strutted into the kitchen.

"What's up, Pops?" Jack asked, before looking to Stevie. "I heard you tore it up yesterday."

Stevie nodded to his older brother before digging into a plate with some eggs, a few pieces of bacon and fruit salad. He swallowed his first bite.

"Yeah?" Stevie said. "Where'd you hear that?"

Jack pointed to the newspaper in Wilton's hand.

"Just a little somethin', somethin'," Stevie said, biting down on a crisp piece of bacon.

Jack smiled as he grabbed a plate. At twenty-five,

he still had the lean, toned body of an athlete, though he'd been out of the game for three years. Jack worked out with Stevie during the summertime and also played in pick-up basketball games at the east Austin YMCA three times a week.

Wilton folded the newspaper and put it down next to his plate. "Was the electrician there this morning?" he asked Jack.

"Yeah, I let him in an hour ago," Jack replied, before popping a piece of bacon into his mouth. "Dennis is in the office making sure it all gets fixed."

Jack was the manager over at Wilton's car dealership. He had followed in Wilton's footsteps by graduating college with a degree in marketing and business administration. Jack landed a job in Memphis after matriculation, giving Tennessee a shot for three years, before deciding to come home to Texas.

Wilton was relieved that Jack had the goods to make it out on his own if necessary and that he wasn't forced to bring his eldest son back to Austin to help run the family business out of desperation.

"Good," Wilton said, with a nod of approval.

Jack fixed himself a plate, and the family proceeded to eat their breakfast without much conversation. The quiet was all Ebony needed to know her family was satisfied. She loved these moments when the family could all be together under one roof. With Wilton and Jack working long hours at the dealership and Stevie devoting so much of his time to football, she knew to cherish these times together.

"So, Stevie," Jack said, after wiping his mouth with a napkin, "you still with that—what's her name? Kendra?"

"Quit playing, man."

"Nah, I'm serious," Jack continued. "You remember her, Pops? Girl was so tall, I thought she was a defensive end. And didn't she have a mustache?"

The whole table cracked, but Stevie didn't take offense. This was the McCrae table—everybody making jokes. The one thing you couldn't be in the

McCrae family was sensitive. You had to have thick skin and had to be able to take it as well as you could dish it out.

"Don't get me started on some of these girls I've seen you running around with," Stevie said. "Dad, he had this one a few months ago. I swear to God, she was big. Like, *real* big. Jack must've been paying for three when they went out to dinner."

That crack got a bigger laugh out of the table than Jack's did. Jack busted up and started laughing himself.

"Seriously," Jack said, after the laughter had subsided. "Do you have a girl?"

Stevie played with his eggs before coming out with it. "Actually, yeah. I just met her a couple of days ago. Seems like I've known her for longer, though."

"She got a name?"

"Yeah. Her name is Madison."

Jack smiled. "Stop playing, man? What's her real name?"

"I just told you."

"She's white?"

"Yeah."

Jack looked at his mother and then father. "What do you guys think?"

Wilton shrugged his shoulders.

Ebony leaned over and rubbed Stevie's hand. "As long as she makes you happy, we don't care what color she is," she said

"Does *Madison* go to your school?" Jack asked in a serious tone.

"Yeah."

"What's her family like?"

"I said I just met her," Stevie said. "Why are you so interested?"

Jack didn't answer and just like that, the tenor of the breakfast had shifted to tense. Jack stared at his little brother while tapping a finger on the edge of his plate.

Ebony looked at Jack with soft eyes and he calmed himself.

Stevie finished his last bite of fruit and stood up

from the table. "I'm gonna go out back and get some fresh air," he said. "Thanks for breakfast, Mom."

"Don't mention it, baby."

Stevie took his plate to the sink and walked through the open patio door that led to the backyard.

Jack wiped his mouth with his napkin again and stood up. He put his plate into the sink before joining his little brother in the back yard.

The McCraes' backyard was large, and the lawn was always freshly manicured. It was in this backyard that Wilton and Jack taught Stevie his first lessons about the game of football—the essential fundamentals of catching, throwing, and tackling. Stevie was sitting on the grass at the edge of the yard as Jack took a seat next to him.

"I remember schooling your little ass out here," Jack said. "You used to run into the house crying any time you skinned a knee."

Stevie didn't reply but thought fondly of those moments growing up. Those were the good days when all he wanted to do was get onto that grass and run. There had been no pressure to break state records or impress scouts. Just Stevie, Wilton, Jack, and a ball.

"Look, I'm not trying to get into your business. I just want to share some knowledge based on my experience," Jack said, taking a soft whack at the back of Stevie's head.

"She's cool," Stevie said. "What difference does it make what color she is?"

"I didn't say she can't be a good person. I'm just saying you should get to know her."

Stevie kept his mouth shut because he knew that if he opened his mouth, the lecture would be prolonged. He knew that Jack wanted the best for him when it came to life and football. Stevie also knew that Jack kept a large chip on his shoulder from his own failed football career, but that never got in the way of the two brothers loving each other.

"You have to watch for these white girls who chase after football players," Jack said.

Stevie thought of the night he met Madison

and couldn't help but think of her friendship with Natasha. That was the only thing about Madison that gave him pause.

"These girls want to trip a brother up," Jack continued. "You can't trust them unless you know what kind of family they come from."

"I told you I just met her. I haven't met her family yet."

"What *do* you know about her?"

"I know that I like her and that she seems trustworthy."

"Does she plan on going to college?"

"She's working to be a chef."

"I thought you said that she was in school."

"She is," Stevie said. "But she also works at one of those farm-to-table joints near UT's campus. She works weekends and a couple of nights a week."

"Hmm," Jack said.

"She's a good girl, Jack. I know what you're saying about some of these girls out there. But Madison is not like that."

"Fine, but meet her family. And pay attention to the signs."

"Okay!"

"And another thing. You gotta drop this obsession with UT. There are other schools out there that would be happy to give you a free education. *And* it would do you some good to leave this place for college. You need to grow up."

"Did you come over here just get on my nerves?"

"Hey," Jack said, "this is knowledge I'm imparting on you as your older brother. You don't know anything about how the world works."

"And you do?"

"Hell yes, I do!"

"Sometimes I wish *you* made it to the NFL so I wouldn't have to hear this crap all the time."

"Listen to me!" Jack said, with a solid punch to Stevie's shoulder. "There are more important things in life than football. I'm not saying that you shouldn't try to push your talent all the way."

Stevie's eyes softened.

"I want you to get an education too. Some school is going to give you a scholarship to play football. Some school other than UT. I want you to take *those* offers seriously. Get a degree, a *real* degree, so you have something to fall back on. I'm not saying this because I don't believe in you. I do."

Stevie nodded and Jack stood up.

"Stand up."

Stevie stood up and only reached his older brother's shoulders. *If only I had Jack's height,* Stevie often thought to himself.

"I'm proud of you," Jack said. "You're a damn good player. But you're a good person too. I'm proud to be your brother."

Jack gave his younger brother a hug. Stevie wrapped an arm around his older brother.

"Just promise me you're gonna get to know this girl you're with and get your degree."

"I promise."

6

ANY RUNNING BACK WORTH HIS SALT TAKES PRIDE in his blocking ability, and Stevie was no exception. When he first made it to varsity as a sophomore, pass-blocking—namely, picking up the blitz—was a struggle. The physicality of the task posed enough trouble, without the memorization of the blocking assignments. With old-fashioned hard work in the form of repetition drills, Stevie improved and eventually became adept. Then and only then could he call himself a complete running back.

So it was no surprise that Stevie was chomping at the bit to go first in the blitz pick-up drill that following Monday at practice. This was an important practice, after all. Austin High's opening game of the regular season was Friday night. And who lined up across from Stevie during the first rep of blitz pick up? Jeron Peters.

Jeron had something to prove after his weak showing in Saturday's practice, creating the potential for intrigue within the normally mundane drill. Stevie waited for Coach Moffit to blow the whistle. He knew from experience that Jeron's favorite pass-rush move was the bull rush. Jeron waited too, his imposing frame glistening with sweat in the afternoon sun. Stevie focused on Jeron's hands. They were tense, tipping off that Jeron was, indeed, coming with the bull rush.

The whistle shrilled and Jeron came with two fists right into Stevie's chest. Stevie gave himself a good base to absorb the blow, and his lack of height actually played to his advantage because it helped to create a low center of gravity, neutralizing Jeron's bull rush. On the second whistle, the two team leaders stopped and patted each other on the helmet before going to the end of their respective lines to wait for the next one-on-one confrontation.

The next practice period called for the individual position groups to go off and work on skills specific to their crafts. The offensive linemen practiced their footwork, the linebackers worked on pass-coverage drops, and the cornerbacks and safeties practiced flipping their hips for each specific coverage scheme. All of this solo work would hopefully meld together to form a cohesive attack.

Stevie and the other running backs worked on ball security during their individual period. Stevie rarely fumbled. During two seasons on varsity, he had fumbled twice, losing one of them. In truth, a closer inspection would've revealed that one of the fumbles could've easily been pinned on the quarterback for not handing the ball off cleanly.

The ball-security drills were monotonous yet valuable. One of the drills consisted of a ball carrier running through a gauntlet consisting of the other running backs. As the ball carrier ran through the chute of arms, teammates chopped down at the ball in an effort to dislodge it. Stevie went first and in an illustration of his know-how, doled out punishment while supposedly playing the target. He had a habit of using his elbow as a ball guard while running, and many times an oncoming defender would catch a jolt from a jutting elbow, the kind of bone-on-bone shock that caused the affected body part to go limp then numb. As Stevie took his turns through the gauntlet, this happened, causing the other backs to shake their burning limbs in agony.

For good measure, Stevie forced his backup, Robby Steward, to fumble with a perfectly timed punch from a spot at the end of the gauntlet. Stevie pounced on the fumble, causing Robby to have to run a lap around the practice field as penance.

The next ball-security drill, Stevie's favorite, was the one where a defender holds the ball carrier up while a second defender tries to rip the ball free. During the first go-through, Stevie took the handoff and streaked through the make-believe hole in the defense. The first defender made contact and held him up before the second defender came over to try to punch the ball out. Stevie held the ball in his right arm, securing it against his ribs. With not enough pigskin exposed, the defenders had no chance of ripping, punching, or stripping the ball out. The whistle blew, and Stevie ran back to the where the drill began.

Coach Myers, Austin High's running backs' coach, stepped in to speak before the drill continued.

"See that?" Myers asked the group. "See how Stevie holds it? High and tight. For you young guys, make sure you're watching Stevie close on these drills. There's nothing more important than holding on to the ball when you're a ball carrier."

The other running backs nodded in unison.

The next period at practice was nine-on-seven—a drill in which no passes were thrown, and the offensive goal was to sharpen the team's running game. There wasn't a better part of practice for Stevie. Early in his sophomore year, it was during nine-on-seven that Stevie proved his worth to the team for the first time. He was fourth on the depth chart early that season, and like most young players, the difference in the speed of the game between junior varsity and varsity posed the most difficulty. During the nine-on-seven portion of the Wednesday practice before the third game of his sophomore season, everything clicked. Stevie began seeing the running lanes before they opened up. He accelerated *through* the hole like coach Myers had preached, rather than accelerating before the hole. And most importantly, he became impossible to tackle. His teammates either bounced off him when he lowered his shoulders, or they grasped at air when he made himself skinny in the hole. By the end of that Wednesday practice Stevie had risen to second on the depth chart, and it didn't take him long to claim the number one running-back spot.

Now, as Austin's undisputed number one back, Stevie waited for the first snap of nine-on-seven, under much different circumstances. The one thing that did not change, however, was his pre-snap routine. He still scanned the defense with discernment, aiming to predict whether the intended hole would open up, or if some improvisation would be necessary. All this happened before he even *touched* the ball. He had almost to assume that the blocking on a given play would be bad because that knowledge would enable him to survive. He didn't feel safe letting his guard down because the second he did so, the threat of a 210-pound outside linebacker coming out of nowhere loomed.

Muretti snapped the ball and handed it to Stevie going left. Stevie saw the hole close up and could *feel* the defense converge. He bounced it outside and saw a sliver of space open at the edge. He ran through one arm tackle before the pursuing defenders, led by Jeron, gang-tackled him for a gain of three. Jeron helped Stevie off the turf.

"Not today, baby!" Jeron barked. "This is a new day!"

"We'll see," Stevie said.

On the next play, Stevie took a handoff going toward the right sideline. In a real game, Stevie tried to avoid as much contact as possible. He was fast and agile enough to head off most of the direct shots running backs dread. But on this play, Stevie wanted to send a message to his team.

As Jeron pursued the play on the backside, Stevie eyed him. He knew that Jeron would come screaming across the field to deliver a blow. Stevie cut on a dime, leaving one defender in the dust. As Jeron neared, Stevie dipped his left shoulder and delivered a blow into the linebacker's chest. Jeron flew off of his feet and hit the field with a thud. Austin's players—both on the field and the sideline—reacted to the jolt. The coaches gushed inwardly at the fire in Stevie's belly. By the time the play was finished, Stevie was in the end zone, and Jeron was being helped up by a teammate. When he returned to the huddle, Stevie flipped the ball to his coach with a wink.

Jeron cleared the cobwebs, and after regaining focus, scanned for Stevie.

Stevie caught the gaze and stood firm.

Instead of reacting with anger, a curious smile appearing on Jeron's face.

Stevie liked that. He wasn't trying to hurt anyone, let alone his own teammate and friend. Stevie was on a mission. He wanted everyone to know that this was his year. He wasn't going to take a snap off, nor was he going to take it easy on anyone, even his teammates.

Stevie smiled back at Jeron and gave him a thumbs-up. Coach Myers put Steward in on the third snap of nine-on-seven before throwing an arm around Stevie's shoulder.

"You might wanna ease up, just a little bit," Coach Myers said, pinching his thumb and pointer finger together. "Seeing as our first game is Friday. We don't need anyone getting hurt before then."

"Just needed to show I mean business," Stevie said before taking a swig from a water bottle.

"Son, *everyone* knows that."

Stevie ran back into the huddle for the fifth snap. The call was Stevie's favorite play: the off-tackle run to the right. Jeron was back in the drill too—ready to exact revenge on Stevie. Muretti called out his cadence, his chest out, swaggering, with an authority that stemmed from handing off to Stevie McCrae.

On the snap, Stevie exploded. He took the ball and burst through the hole. At the second level, he stiff-armed an oncoming defender and broke through to the secondary. Once there, a safety came over to slow him down. The safety wrapped his arms around Stevie's hips, but he would not go down. As Stevie fought for extra yardage, two pursuing defenders arrived to get him on the ground. Most backs would call it a day at this point, but not Stevie. He wanted every inch. When the two defenders climbed onto his back, Stevie decided that he would finally go down—that *this* was the threshold between gutsy and stupid. Problem was, a fourth defender hustled over at the last moment and jumped onto the totem pole that was Stevie's back. The sheer weight caused the ankle to give out.

7

THE PROGNOSIS WAS NEITHER POSITIVE NOR crushing. The ACL and the rest of the knee were intact. The leg as a whole was stable. Stevie had suffered the dreaded high ankle sprain on his left foot, however. An everyday sprained ankle would have been less worrisome. Stevie had turned both ankles countless times. The high ankle sprain was a trickier and more painful proposition, and though called a "sprain," the tiny tears in the ankle ligaments belied a murkier recovery period than its cousin, the garden-variety ankle sprain. Hence the internal bleeding, causing swelling and pain.

"How long?" Stevie asked, in the trainer's room, with his left foot in a bucket of ice. Every now and then there was a shot of pain from the damage, causing his eyes to narrow and his breath to deepen.

Austin's trainer, Robert Kincaid, knew Stevie. He knew Stevie would contest any period of recovery placed on his foot. But it was Kincaid's job to tell the truth.

"On the low end," Kincaid said, "four weeks."

As soon as the words left Kincaid's mouth, Stevie began shaking his head.

"On the high end, eight weeks."

"I'm not sitting out for eight weeks!" Stevie yelled. He took a deep breath and then looked into Kincaid's eyes. "I'll heal quicker than that."

Kincaid didn't respond. Injuries create moments fraught with tension. Kincaid needed to take the emotion out of the situation. Responding to Stevie would do the opposite.

"Not eight weeks," Stevie repeated, unprompted.

"We can get you back to full strength," Kincaid said. "We're just gonna need time."

"I don't have time."

"You do. You're young."

"No. You don't get it. This season is my chance. I can't count on anything else but *this* season."

It was Kincaid's turn to take a deep breath before patting Stevie on the back. Though difficult, he stuck to his rule of showing as little emotion as possible after a serious injury. It's what Stevie needed. "Coach wants to talk to you, Stevie. I'll go grab him. Hang in there, okay?"

Kincaid left the door cracked open behind him, leaving a sliver of a portal to the locker room. On normal days after practice, the locker room was a place of exhilaration and comedy. But on this day, it more resembled a funeral procession as Austin's players showered and changed in silence. It went without saying that Stevie's teammates understood the magnitude of his potential loss. The players left the locker room little by little until it became church-quiet inside. A collective breath was held as a season of promise was now in jeopardy.

Coach Moffit entered the trainer's room and placed a hand on Stevie's left shoulder. "How are you feeling?"

Stevie winced as he reconfigured his foot in the ice bucket. It had already puffed up with a welt the size of a baseball.

"I knew it was bad when it happened. Kincaid says it's bad."

Coach Moffit didn't comment. Unlike Kincaid, he held eye contact with Stevie.

"Just let me see how I feel in a day or two, before you rule me out for Friday's game," Stevie said, his optimistic nature already starting to come to the surface.

"You want to try to play on *Friday*?" Coach Moffit asked. "This Friday?"

"Hell yeah."

"Stevie, Kincaid said 'weeks' not 'days.'"

"I know what he said. Four weeks if all goes well.

Most of the season if it doesn't. But I'm not going to accept that."

Moffit had seen a lot in twenty years of coaching high school football. What he hadn't seen, was a player who was this confident, and apparently clear-headed after a serious injury. His years of experience told him what to say next.

"Stevie, this isn't an ankle tweak. You're lucky actually. It looked like a season-ender when it happened. I just thank God that your left leg didn't snap in two."

"Me too," Stevie said, "but I'm here in one piece. This won't stop me."

"Stop you from what, son? You don't have a single thing to prove. To anyone." He put both hands on Stevie's shoulders and looked his star running back dead in the eye.

This was what Stevie loved about his coach—he was a straight shooter. Stevie had heard stories of duplicitous coaches all around the state of Texas, but Coach Moffit was not one of those.

"You cannot let the University of Texas dictate your worth. You are going to go off and play college football somewhere. And you are going to give it all you have. You'll be a dynamic, productive player out on the field. Your road is long. This is just a small bump. That's all it is."

Stevie smiled. Not because he had heard this speech before. He wasn't too talented or jaded for the words of inspiration that permeated the institution of football. He smiled because Coach Moffit did not get it. Stevie *had* to play for the University of Texas. There was not another option.

"Coach, it's a challenge. There's no way I could live with myself if I backed down from it. And this," Stevie chin nodded his swollen appendage down in the bucket, "it's only gonna make my story sweeter."

Moffit smiled like a father who loved his son but did not approve of the choice his progeny had made. "Okay," he said, "but you're not playing this week. We'll reevaluate you next Monday. We'll examine you then and see, I repeat *see,* about the second game of the season."

It was hard for Stevie to agree to that, and he knew how hard it would be to stand on the sideline during the first game of the season, but he had to agree to this. He knew his foot was a mess, but with a full week off? *Let's see what happens,* he thought.

"One other thing," Moffit said. "Can you just go down when there are three people on your back? This whole thing could've been avoided if you would have just gone down."

"It's not in me to play it that way, Coach," Stevie said with a shrug. "I only know one speed."

"You're killing me, McCrae."

· ·

Stevie shared the news of his injury with Madison before anyone else. He called her after he finished icing his foot. She volunteered to come back to school and give him a ride home.

Stevie was on crutches as he waited in the parking lot behind school. Madison arrived and got out to help him into the passenger seat. They kissed briefly, naturally, on the lips upon sight of one another. Jack's words popped into Stevie's mind as Madison pulled the car out of the school's lot, but he quickly dismissed them. He didn't see Madison as opportunistic. Their interactions were pleasant and seamless. Besides, they were both passionate and driven about their pursuits. The business of their individual lives created a smooth ground for their genuine relationship. They were not on the phone with each other all the time as many smitten high schoolers were. Nor were they all over each other physically. That's not to say that Stevie was not interested in Madison physically. There simply hadn't been ample opportunity with their demanding schedules. Madison wanted to be with Stevie, too, and she knew the question of sex would soon pop-up.

"Wanna eat something?" Madison asked. "There's

this new Korean barbecue place near campus that's supposed to be hot."

"I could eat."

Madison made a detour and headed toward UT. The campus was flooded with students as the fall semester was about to commence. The bustling area also served those who had no affiliation to the university, the principal reason being that the best restaurants in Austin were situated on the grounds of the University of Texas.

Madison dropped Stevie off in front of the restaurant, and it was clear that she hadn't overstated the joint's popularity. A line had started from inside that spilled out the front door and snaked around the corner. Madison parked a few blocks away and met Stevie out front.

"Sorry. I couldn't go inside and put our names on the list," he said, nodding to his crutches.

"It's okay," she said, pulling out her cell phone.

She typed a text and sent it off. Three minutes later, she received a response that caused her to smile.

The door to the restaurant opened and a thin, mustachioed man, with both arms covered in tattoos, looked out to the sidewalk. Madison caught his gaze. He smiled.

"Uh, Madison for two," he called out, theatrically.

"Yes, that's us," she said, leaning into it.

Madison helped Stevie inside and the tattooed man led them to two seats at the bar. The smells caused Stevie's jowls to water—the charred whiff of grilled meats, the faint, vinegary perfume of pickles. Madison gave the tattooed man a fist bump before helping Stevie onto a stool. She settled onto a stool next to him.

"You're a good person to know," Stevie said.

"Comes from working in restaurants," she said. "You make a lot of friends."

Stevie looked at his girlfriend with wonder. Madison aroused him physically as well as mentally. She could actually *do* something. She wasn't just a pretty face.

He looked around the restaurant and saw other

couples and packs of friends that were mixed. The race thing didn't matter to him. His parents never talked to him about race. The only person who did was his brother Jack. Racial harmony didn't seem to bother many people in Austin either. True, this was Texas, and Stevie was black and Madison white, but like the tenor of their relationship, Austin was different.

"I'm glad you brought me here."

"The food smells amazing," she said with indulgence. "Do you like kimchi?"

"I don't know what that is, but if you say it's good, I'm sure it is."

Madison smiled and when the waiter arrived, she did all the ordering, as usual. She ordered a special kind of grilled steak that they'd share along with a variety of Korean pickles. As Stevie observed Madison while she ordered, he realized just how beautiful she was. Her independent, self-confident nature only added to this beauty. He fought every urge to say something corny like, "Madison, you're really something." Stevie just let the moment pass between them, thinking how much he liked this girl, and how he hoped she liked him as much.

When the pickles arrived, Stevie was jarred by their pungency up close.

"I know the smell is intense," she said. "Some of it smells like rotting trash. But believe me." She took her chopsticks and dug out a piece of what looked like cabbage covered in a red paste. She put the bite in her mouth and closed her eyes. "It *is* delicious."

Stevie grabbed his chopsticks and took a piece of the cabbage. He held his breath and took the bite. It was aggressively seasoned with garlic, but Madison was right. It was delicious.

"Wait'll you try it with the meat," she said.

"I know," he said. "I can smell it."

A bit of silence passed between them as Madison went in for another bite. She wiped her mouth with the napkin in her lap, and her eyes moved down to Stevie's heavily wrapped ankle.

"That looks pretty serious, Stevie," Madison said.

"It is."

"Are you playing Friday?"

Stevie winced as he adjusted his sitting position. "Not Friday, but I'm gonna try to get back out there for the second game."

"You seem so calm about it."

Stevie didn't reply. He just smiled.

"I mean, because of your plans and all," she said.

He shrugged. "What can I do? It sucks that I got injured a few days before the first game of the season. But I'll be back."

"You're not afraid?"

"No."

The food arrived. Madison took in the smell of the sizzling meat cooked to medium rare.

"Okay," she said. "Take a piece of steak and then some rice."

Stevie did so.

"And then take some of the pickled stuff and put it on top."

Madison modeled this for him. She grabbed a

little bit of everything with her chopsticks and took the bite. The look on her face as she chewed was ecstasy. "The perfect bite," she said.

* *

Madison drove Stevie home and they sat out in front of his house in her car for a while. They kissed with the tacit enthusiasm of wanting to do more.

"Listen, Stevie," she said, breathing deeply after a passionate flurry. "I want you to know that I would like to do it."

"I know that. And I want you to know that I want to do it, too."

"I'm not a prude, but I didn't want to do it after the first couple of times we hung out. You know? I wanted it to feel right."

"I understand."

"I'm ready now. It feels right."

She sighed as Stevie kissed her neck.

"Me too," he said, pulling away. "I mean, sort of.

My stupid foot would make it difficult. I wouldn't be able to move around much."

Madison chuckled.

"What?" Stevie asked.

"It's funny."

"Yeah. It is funny. Not being able to have sex because of a football injury."

They both laughed.

"It's okay," she said, kissing him on the forehead. "When you heal up, you'll have something besides football to look forward to."

8

STEVIE DID NOT PRACTICE ON TUESDAY, Wednesday, or Thursday of that week.

Tuesday was a recovery day. Stevie was still on crutches, and it was out of the question to dump them. He received permission from all of his teachers to complete his classwork in the trainer's room, and that allowed Kincaid to treat him all day. He also did treatment while the team practiced after school.

There was a prescribed repetition used in an effort to get the swelling down: ice, heat, stimulation. Icing was the hardest for Stevie; his ankle was sore to the touch, meaning that the very mention of the word "ice" raised the hair on the back of his neck. When the ubiquitous ice pack actually hit the raw ankle, a buzz of pain made a beeline to Stevie's brain and then sent its charges throughout his entire body. Heat provided relief. The heat's purpose was to sooth the damaged joint and ligaments, and it did so with efficacy.

The last stage of rehab was EMS, as in electronic muscle stimulation. Stim was used on an injured player to create muscle contractions in the weakened area. By adhering to this last step, a rehabbing player could get additional blood flow to the injured spot. The stim machine didn't bother Stevie from a pain standpoint. It was just boring.

Stevie had gone through the ice-heat-stim pattern six times by the time school let out on Tuesday. When practice began, he started his eighth cycle. Sitting in the trainer's room while his teammates were out on the field was as painful as the actual injury. But Stevie knew the injury would not heal fast enough on its own. This was the only way. By

Tuesday's end, Stevie felt a slight difference in his bum wheel. It was tender, and he couldn't yet let go of the crutches, but there was progress. Stevie was sure of it.

During the first half of Wednesday, the routine was more or less the same as the day before. Ice. Heat. Stim. After lunch, Stevie asked Kincaid if he could walk in an attempt to get the stiffness out and range of motion back into the injured ankle. Kincaid grudgingly agreed but told Stevie that at the first sign of pain, he would have to get off the foot. Before Stevie attempted a step, Kincaid massaged the ankle and warned him of the rawness still inside. Stevie heeded the warning but was ready to give walking a try.

The first step felt as if a plate of glass had been shattered on his ankle, and the resulting shards were stuck inside his skin. Stevie hid the pain on his face with a look of determination. The display fooled Kincaid well enough. After a few paces back and forth in the trainer's room, the limb loosened up and so did the pain. A wave of happiness washed over Stevie. But Kincaid was quick to remind him that there was a lot more progress to be made. Nonetheless, a good first step.

At Wednesday's end, the ankle felt markedly better. Stevie tried to convince Kincaid to let him go home without crutches, but this request was one that the trainer could not and would not grant.

Stevie felt like a million bucks when he woke up Thursday morning. The swelling was down by seventy-five percent. He made the unilateral decision to chuck the crutches, leaving them in a heap in his garage before catching a ride to school with Madison. His limp was minimal, only visible to the informed or hyper-discerning eye. There would be no way of convincing Kincaid and Coach Moffit to let him play on Friday, but a return for game number two looked promising.

When he arrived at school, Kincaid scolded him for not using the crutches. Stevie showed him his ankle and to Kincaid's amazement, Stevie's considerable swelling had gone down faster than any player he had ever seen in his years at the school. This development propelled Stevie to work even harder that day. He hit the ice, heat, and stim routine during the first half of the day, and after lunch, received a massage, and walked around the basketball gym under Kincaid's watchful eye.

"I don't know how the hell you are walking around right now," Kincaid said.

"Power of positive thinking, baby!"

"I really can't believe this."

Stevie and Kincaid walked back to the trainer's room.

"Is it loose?" Kincaid asked.

Stevie sat down on one of the table's used as a taping station before practices and games.

"Yes," Stevie said.

Kincaid began kneading Stevie's ankle. It was no longer tender, and Stevie could feel the strength coming back into the joint.

"Can I go on the field and run?"

"No way, Stevie."

"I'm telling you the truth. I feel fine."

"Not yet. We agreed on Monday."

"Yeah, but we *agreed* on Monday with the thought that I'd be nowhere near ready to play."

"No."

With no other cards to play, Stevie did what he was told. More boredom, more repetition. Ice. Heat. Stim. He would not complain though. He was way past that, already envisioning a dominating performance in game two. He just needed his teammates to come through for him in that first game. He had to lead Austin High to an undefeated season and state championship. That was the only way he'd get UT's attention. With his foot well on its way to recovery, the thought of his destiny being out of his hands was the only source of uneasiness.

On the Friday morning of the first game of the season, Stevie went back to class with the rest of his classmates. His ankle had improved to the point of no longer needing around-the-clock rehab. Many of Austin High's students sent him well wishes, both in class and when he passed by them without a limp in the hallway.

Austin High's first game of the season was at home against McNeil High School, a team outside of Austin's district. Though the two schools did not face off annually, tensions were high due to McNeil's and Austin's physical proximity. McNeil would travel sixteen miles south to face Austin High, bringing an experienced and physical squad that had made it to the playoffs the season before.

Stevie entered the locker room after school. Before doing anything else, he stopped at the locker of his backup, Robby Steward, who looked calm and collected, albeit with a bubbling inside his gut. Steward's first-ever start would be under the Friday night lights, against a legitimate Texas high school team. Stevie knew what was going through his understudy's mind.

"Just tuck that thing high and tight," Stevie said. "You'll be fine."

"Thanks," Robby said. "How's your foot?"

Stevie smiled. "Let's just say that this is a one-week job for you."

Steward smiled and rubbed at the scruff forming around his chin.

Stevie figured that while he had Steward's attention, he would impart a little knowledge. "On the dive plays, just hit it up in there and get as much yardage as you can. They're big up front, so you shouldn't expect a lot of holes," Stevie said.

Steward nodded.

"Do your thing out there tonight," Stevie said, and the two backs shook hands.

Stevie went on to his own locker and dropped his bag off. His game jersey hung inside, but he would not wear it on the sideline. Jerseys were for active players. A black T-shirt and jeans would have to do.

Stevie knocked on the door to Coach Moffit's office.

"Coach."

"Yeah, come on in, Stevie."

Stevie walked in to find his coach at his desk, looking over his play sheet. Stevie took a seat.

"No limp," Moffit observed.

"I feel good."

"Tonight's gonna be tough sledding without you. Young quarterback. Backup running back."

"I wish I could be out there tonight."

"I know you do."

"I'll be ready for next week. There's no doubt."

"I know you've lived in that trainer's room this past week," Moffit said, with a smile.

"I wanted to play tonight."

"It's the right move. Come Monday we'll check you out and if everything's clear, you'll play."

"Okay."

Stevie got up from the chair.

"One more thing, Stevie. If things aren't going

well out there tonight, I want you to lift the guys up. You're so used to being out there and *doing* things. I know it'll be different. But the guys look up to you."

"Sure thing, Coach."

"Who knows? Maybe your being out tonight will help the team in the long run. Force us to throw the ball a little more."

"I'll help as much as I can."

Stevie left his coach's office and reentered the locker room. The space was now filled with the enthusiastic sounds and movements indicative of the hope that comes with a new football season—the hope that is echoed in many cities across the state of Texas, as Friday night approaches.

. . . .

Austin High's field was immaculate before kickoff. This was not lost on Stevie as he walked around the field a few hours before. The sun was beginning its descent, and the lights were just chugging to life above. Stevie loved the feel of an empty football field before a game. The silence moved him and reinforced the belief that *here, in this space* was where he belonged.

Slowly, players and coaches from both teams began populating the field. After that, the stands on both sides filled out with supporters. The lights overhead shone brightly and proudly now. Music—mostly hip-hop—blared as well. Players on both sides bobbed their heads to the syncopated lyrics blaring out of the PA. Stevie allowed himself to curse the fact that he'd have to miss the opening game one final time.

McNeil High's players were as large as advertised. The cross-town squad was imposing in both height and girth. Seeing McNeil's physicality up close inspired a last-minute thought in Stevie's mind, a thought he'd dispense to Robby Steward. He walked over to where Steward and the rest of the running backs were catching passes.

Stevie pulled Steward aside. "You gotta get low

on those inside runs tonight," he said. "I know you think you're Eric Dickerson and try to run high like him. But that's not going to work. Not tonight. You have to get low against these big boys."

Steward looked over to where McNeil's defensive linemen were warming up on the other end of the field.

"Their d-line is tall," Stevie continued. "It's gonna be hard for them to get low enough to stop you from digging out those extra yards."

"Yeah that makes sense," Robby said. "I appreciate it."

"If you stay low."

Steward nodded and the two shook hands. Steward went back to warming up, and Stevie took a deep breath. The opening kickoff was nearing. He left the field and took a prime spot on the sideline near Coach Moffit. Stevie didn't have anything left to give but his support. It was going to be up to his teammates on the field. His grand plan was in the hands of others, and now that the game had actually arrived, it killed him.

. . . .

Austin High won the coin toss and chose to receive. The opening kick sailed through the end zone, and Austin's offense started the game from its own twenty. Muretti got underneath center for the opening play. The formation showed power: two backs, two tight ends, and a receiver. But instead of handing it off to Steward, Muretti dropped back and lofted a pass to Austin's number one receiver, Teddy Fales, who ran a go route down the right sideline.

Fales caught the pass in stride and would've scored if it hadn't been for the shoestring tackle made by McNeil's free safety. The play went for fifty yards and set up Austin High with a first down at McNeil's thirty-yard line.

As Austin's crowd rejoiced, Stevie looked at his

coach. In previous seasons, Austin would never have started a game with a deep pass as the big plays always came from Stevie. Coach Moffit returned Stevie's glance with a knowing look of his own.

On the second play from scrimmage, Muretti handed the ball off to Steward on an inside dive, and as Stevie had predicted, there was not much push from Austin's offensive line. Steward took Stevie's pre-game note and applied it, getting low while churning out as many yards as possible. The result was a gain of three yards.

A sweep to the right was the call on play three. This time, there was more room on the outside, and Steward juked one defender and lowered his shoulder on another for a gain of twelve. Austin High was at McNeil's fifteen when, on the next play, Muretti dropped back and found his tight end, Wally Fernandez, in the middle of the end zone.

Stevie was first to greet Muretti as the QB reached the sideline. He couldn't hear Stevie because the cheering section behind Austin's bench would not allow it. The home crowd sensed the magnitude of the touchdown pass. With a real quarterback, the possibilities for the season seemed endless.

"Those yards are earned, not given!" Stevie yelled to Steward over the din.

Steward nodded and the two running backs shook hands.

It was time for the defense to make a statement, and time for Jeron to wreak havoc on McNeil High.

Whereas McNeil's defense was a collection of giants, its offense was the opposite. McNeil's quarterback, Donnie Cortez, was undersized and led an attack predicated on speed. McNeil boasted a talented troop of skilled position players that were quick, stout, and interchangeable.

On McNeil's first play, Jeron made the tackle on a dive up the middle. On second down, McNeil went to the air and gashed Austin High with a well-timed screen pass to its slot receiver. The play went for forty yards, down to Austin's twenty-five. Jeron missed an arm tackle on the play, opening up an avenue for the big gain.

Jeron didn't look right to Stevie. Even during preseason practice, something seemed off. Stevie wasn't sure if it was an injury holding Jeron back. One thing Stevie did know was that if Austin High was going to make it far in the playoffs, Jeron would have to play up to his standard, at the very least.

Two downs later, McNeil capped its opening drive with a twenty-yard touchdown pass by Cortez. Austin's crowd sat silent as McNeil kicked the ball through the uprights and knotted the score at seven.

Austin High's defense left the field deflated. Stevie thought about asking Jeron if he was okay, but decided against it. He did not want to get into Jeron's head while the linebacker was in the thick of the action. Stevie was familiar with the frequent annoyance of being questioned or criticized by someone who was not in the game. A one-on-one talk with Jeron would have to wait until a more appropriate time. Instead, a firm pat on the back was all Stevie offered to his friend.

As each team's defense gained its footing and adjusted to what the opposing offense was doing, Austin's ensuing drive ended with a three and out, and McNeil's second drive followed suit.

With three minutes left in the first half, Austin took possession of the ball at its own thirty-yard line with the score still tied. Muretti dropped back to pass. Due to quick pressure coming from the right side, Muretti's mechanics faltered, and he nearly threw an interception that would've likely been returned for a touchdown. Luckily, McNeil's defensive back allowed the errant pass to hit him in the numbers rather than catching it with his hands. On second down, Steward took a toss sweep and ripped off a forty-yard gain down the left sideline—Austin's most substantial gain since its opening drive.

Though the clock ticked below two minutes, Coach Moffit urged his team to take its time. McNeil's large defense was gassed, but Coach

Moffit wanted to ensure that McNeil would not get another possession before halftime. Muretti got the message and let the clock dwindle before leading the offense to the line of scrimmage. Austin's deliberate approach was moot because on the next play, Muretti was flushed from the pocket, and instead of throwing the ball away, the young quarterback held on to it a second too long. A pursuing defensive end sacked Muretti and chopped down on his arm in the process. Muretti lost the ball, and it bounced once off the turf and right into the waiting arms of McNeil's outside linebacker. Stevie was helpless as the linebacker ran past him and down Austin's sideline for a touchdown.

Austin High trailed fourteen to seven going into the locker room for halftime, where the team was feeling a collective shell shock. The good vibes from the opening possession had vanished into the ether. To Stevie, the Muretti touchdown pass felt like it was from another game, from a distant season. He racked his brain for the solution; his teammates would be rattled, and the halftime break would do nothing but stoke those nervous yips and shakes in the bellies of Austin's players.

Coach Moffit called out one of his favorite football maxims as he followed his team off the field and into the locker room: "Football is a game that can be fickle. You can never take it for granted that the other team will simply lie down after you lean on them a little bit." The platitude echoed in the tunnel leading to Austin's locker room.

9

THE SPACE INSIDE THE LOCKER ROOM WAS SILENT. Coach Moffit huddled with his offensive and defensive coordinators briefly before observing his team. This felt like an important moment for his squad, even though the season had only just begun.

Stevie, in turn, watched Coach Moffit. The injured foot left Stevie voiceless. Rather than stay there and stew amid the sea of frustration in the locker room, he left and headed back out to the field before the rest of his team. He had nothing to offer but more frustration. He had no urge to butt in with suggestions. That was a job for the coaches. Stevie knew better than anyone that when you're in it, really *in* it, and the bullets are flying for real, it's best to have a mind that is free to react.

Willingness to improvise was one of Stevie's finest qualities on the field. True, he watched more film than anyone else on the team, but some of his best work over the seasons came from *being* out there and simply reacting. "An openness to alternate paths" is what his father had called it after Stevie's exceptional touchdown run toward the end of his sophomore season. Once the phrase was coined, Stevie embraced the mantra fully and stuck to it as one of his guiding principles. Now, his teammates had to figure their own paths to "openness" on the field without any further pressing from himself. He knew their brains were already inundated with Xs and Os and adjustments.

Coach Moffit did not speak until his star player left. Like Stevie, he too recognized that the fight Austin High was in would be difficult to overcome without its best player. To survive and keep its hopes alive for a special season, Austin would have to be much better in the second half.

"Bring it up, guys!" Coach Moffit called out.

The team tightened around him in an ill-formed circle.

Stevie paced the sidelines right before the second half kickoff with no sense as to what the outcome of the contest would be. He only knew what was at stake: an undefeated season, a state championship, and a scholarship to UT.

McNeil received the kick and started play from its own twenty-five yard line. On the first snap of the second half, Jeron darted into the backfield and tackled McNeil's running back for a loss of five. The linebacker urged the crowd on before the referee warned him for excessive celebration. On second down, McNeil's quarterback, Cortez, threw a screen pass to his back, which Jeron snuffed out for a gain of five. McNeil was faced with third and ten and a three and out was exactly what Austin High needed.

Cortez took the shotgun snap and Jeron came on a well-timed blitz up the middle. He powered through the running back's block attempt with a bull-rush and sacked Cortez for a loss of ten.

As the defense came off the field, Stevie gave spirited handshakes to every member but saved a a chest bump for Jeron. In that succession of plays, Jeron resembled the player Stevie knew, a player who flew around the field, raising the level of his teammates. Austin High fielded the punt and started its drive right across midfield, at McNeil's forty-seven.

Muretti looked over McNeil's defense at the line of scrimmage before snapping the ball on first down. The play was designed as an off-tackle run to the right. The problem was, Muretti turned the wrong way after the snap and was tackled for a loss of five. Stevie bit his lower lip on the sideline. He was all too familiar with the growing pains associated with playing a young quarterback. Muretti's mistake couldn't have come at a worse time as Austin's offensive footing was slipping.

Muretti was lucky that he didn't throw a pick-six referee on the second down. Faced with heavy pressure up the middle, he panicked and threw the ball up into the air, amongst a sea of McNeil's defenders. Two McNeil defenders went up for the ball at the same time and crashed into one another. The ball fell inexplicably to the turf. Austin was faced with third and fifteen.

Coach Moffit called a timeout before the play. "Stevie!" he yelled.

Stevie approached as Muretti neared the sideline. The quarterback's chest was thumping, and his jitters were real, not some imaginary ghosts hanging over him from the pressure of the moment. Stevie put a hand on his back.

"You okay?" Coach Moffit asked Muretti.

"Yeah," Muretti said. "A lot of quick pressure and its coming from everywhere."

"You gotta see the 'hots,'" coach Moffit said. "I know there's not a whole lot of time to think out there, but you have to trust the offense and pull the trigger."

Muretti nodded as he tried to catch his breath.

Coach Moffit turned to Stevie. "What do you think?"

"About what?" Stevie replied.

"Well, what do you see?"

Stevie had given his unsolicited suggestions on which plays to run in the past, but was never *asked* to give his thoughts on what play should be called. This was a large gap that Stevie was staring into.

"Coach . . . I . . . "

"No time for that," he said. "I trust you."

Openess, Stevie thought.

"Outside of the first drive, our only success has come from attacking the edges," Stevie said, his brain pushing out the words quicker than his mouth could grasp them. The instinct was sound because there wasn't much left of the timeout. "A screen pass would probably work, maybe 90-jailbreak? Get Steward free in space."

Coach Moffit nodded in agreement. When the referee blew his whistle from on the field, ending the stoppage, he then looked at Muretti.

"Make sure you *see* a lane to throw the screen to Steward," he said. "If not, put it in the dirt."

Muretti nodded and ran back onto the field and into the huddle.

Stevie bent over and placed both hands on his knees, watching the body language of his team on the field, as it faced the long odds of third and fifteen. Muretti snapped the ball. The offensive lineman held their blocks for a beat. Then, in unison, they allowed McNeil's defenders to charge into the backfield. The screen pass was set up to perfection, if only Muretti could get the ball to Steward. A lane parted between two McNeil defenders, and Muretti was able to shovel the pass to Steward.

Steward snagged the ball out of the air with one hand and saw nothing but grass. He followed the clearing his lineman had set down the right sideline and crossed into the end zone untouched. Stevie exhaled and pumped both fists, as Austin's kicker put the extra point through the uprights, tying the score at fourteen.

Austin High kicked the ball off, and a good return set McNeil up at midfield. Coach Moffit kicked the dirt at his team's shoddy special teams' play. On first down, McNeil gashed Austin's defense with a jet-sweep to the left, which gained thirty-five yards. Jeron missed a tackle on the play, and just like that, the defense was in the shadow of its own goal post.

Cortez allowed the third quarter clock to run out before running another play.

Each member of Austin's defense came over to the sideline holding up four fingers. Stevie and the rest of his teammates followed suit. The game entered the fourth quarter, the time for a team's brightest stars to shine. These players knew who they were by instinct alone. Holding up four fingers was a call to action. When healthy, Stevie was a player who never shied away from the action. He held up his four fingers and stared at Jeron. *This* was the linebacker's moment to do something for his team.

On the first play of the fourth, Austin's defense stepped up with a huge play in the secondary. Due to lack of pressure from Austin's defensive front, Cortez had enough time to scan the entire field for an open receiver, until he found one he liked in the back-right corner of the end zone. Cortez released the pass, and if wasn't for an outstretched pass breakup by Austin's right cornerback, Jamie Rollins, the play would've resulted in six for McNeil. Stevie leapt into the air at the close call and landed awkwardly, sending a shot of pain through his foot.

The second down play was a run that gained three yards for McNeil. Third and seven, it was the biggest play of the game up to that point. Cortez dropped back, and due to quick inside pressure, he was forced to escape the pocket to the right. When he did, there was a lot of space in front of him. Jeron gave chase from the middle of the field, closing the space and tackling Cortez two yards short of the first down.

Fourth down.

Jeron roared and flexed his arms in Cortez's direction. McNeil sent in its kicker to make the chip shot, giving the visitors a three-point lead. There were seven minutes to go, and although Coach Moffit wanted to stay aggressive, the dilemma of relying on a young quarterback causcd him to vacillate. He knew that his approach for these last seven minutes would go a long way toward either bolstering or shattering his young quarterback's confidence.

Coach Moffit reassured Muretti that the game was still in his hands before sending the quarterback onto the field with the drive's opening play call. The drive began at Austin's forty-five yard line after a good return. First down didn't yield much—Steward ran up the middle for a short gain. The call on second down was another run, this time an off-tackle play to the left. Steward took the handoff from Muretti and saw a small crease open up between the left guard and tackle. He hit the hole with as much oomph as he could muster, but his legs were spent from having never carried the full load before. Robby gained seven yards, setting up third and two.

The clock ticked down to five minutes and change. Austin's offense broke the huddle and walked to the line of scrimmage. Muretti snapped the ball and turned to hand it to Steward once again. McNeil's defensive lineman shot their gaps and stormed the backfield. Steward was tackled for a loss of three.

Coach Moffit was left with a major decision to make.

He looked at his sideline. To a man, his players were stunned, sucking away any confidence in a fourth-down gamble. There were four minutes left in the game, and Austin High had all of its timeouts. Coach Moffit decided to punt the ball with the hope that his defense could come up big one more time.

Austin's punter, Donnie King, committed the mortal sin of kicking the ball into the end zone, rather than kicking it high into the air and pinning McNeil deep in its own end. McNeil took possession from its own twenty-yard line. After allowing a seven-yard run on first down, Austin High called its first time out. Second down was a disaster, as McNeil's running back gashed the Maroons' defense for a run of forty yards. As the clock ticked down to two minutes and thirty seconds, Coach Moffit held onto his last two timeouts to see what would happen on the next play. Cortez milked the clock down to two minutes before calling a timeout for McNeil. The ball was at Austin's thirty-seven yard line.

On the first play after the timeout, Jeron stopped McNeil's running back for no gain. Coach Moffit called his second timeout. On second down, Austin's run defense came up with another stop for no gain. Third and final timeout. There was one minute and forty-five seconds left. McNeil would not have to run another play. Their offense could kneel on third down, bleed the clock, and punt it to Austin with somewhere around thirty seconds remaining. That would not be enough time for Austin to drive into McNeil territory for the tying field goal, with an inexperienced quarterback, no less.

After the timeout, Cortez squatted to take the snap, the formation tight, signaling a kneel-down. What happened next will live on in Texas's high school football lore. McNeil's center snapped the ball before Cortez was ready for it. The ball squirted out of the QB's hands and onto the field. Jeron saw the ball before anyone else. He waded through the scrum and in one motion, scooped up the ball and headed the other way. Cortez's quarterback had the presence of mind to sprint after Jeron, and as the linebacker neared the end zone, there wasn't much separation between him and the QB.

Jeron was tripped up at the one-yard line by Cortez, setting up first and goal for Austin High.

Stevie looked up at the scoreboard in disbelief. Thirty seconds remained on the clock. No one—not a player, coach or spectator—could comprehend what they had just seen. The dazed, almost non-existent reaction inside the stadium denoted a scene of mass perplexity.

Coach Moffit shook himself out of his own daze and brought Muretti in close. He gave him the play. Muretti and the rest of Austin's offense went onto the field.

Stevie cracked his knuckles and returned to his hands-on-the-knee pose. At this point, Stevie had no wishes, dreams, or inclinations. He just knew he loved football.

On the very first play, Muretti handed the ball off to Steward on a dive to the left. The offensive line did not get any movement on McNeil's defensive line. Steward knew what he had to do. He went low and plunged into the end zone.

Stevie put both arms into the air, palms open, as his understudy broke the plane. Out of fear that this dream would end, he did not close his eyes until the scoreboard read triple zeros. But after the gun sounded, and Austin had earned the win, Stevie closed his eyes and opened them. His plan was still intact.

10

THE PLAN FOR STEVIE AND JERON WAS TO CELE-brate the victory over dinner with Madison and Natasha. Madison had worked a shift at *The Dutch Oven* that night but still wanted to hang out.

When the two players were dropped off by a teammate at another restaurant that Madison rec-ommended, the two girls were already taking up two stools at a four top near the bar. Jeron and Stevie took the stools next to their respective girls. While Jeron and Natasha started necking, Stevie and Madison kissed softly. Once again, Madison ordered the table.

The food arrived and they ate every single bite with smiles on their faces.

Natasha raised her wine glass, "This is to tonight's big win," Natasha said, "and to Stevie coming back healthy for next week's game."

The four of them clinked glasses and drank. It hadn't occurred to Stevie until then that Madison's glass was filled with water.

"I'm gonna go have a cigarette," Natasha said. "Jeron, come outside and keep me company."

Natasha and Jeron left the table and went outside.

"Hey, I noticed that you don't drink," Stevie said. "What's up with that?"

"Well, I have to thank Natasha for that."

"What do you mean?"

Madison rubbed her neck, which was stiff from standing over her cook station for five hours. Stevie put his hand on the trouble spot and massaged.

"Ooh, that feels good," Madison said. "Well, Natasha helped me stop drinking. I kind of had a problem."

"*Natasha* helped you stop drinking?"

"Yup."

"Wow."

"That's why I'm loyal to her," Madison said. "We're very different now. We used to have similar wants. But now that I don't drink, well, our interests are different."

Stevie nodded his head slowly. It made sense now. He could understand how two people who seemed so different could be friends. There was still one thing he had trouble wrapping his mind around.

"Are you serious though?" he said. "*Natasha* helped you quit drinking? She doesn't seem like the type, and neither do you."

Madison smiled sweetly. The low, golden light of the restaurant glinted in her eyes when she tilted her head.

"You're right," she said. "Natasha isn't the type who'd use 'stop' and 'drinking' in the same sentence. Especially when it comes to herself."

"Crazy," he said.

"But she really helped me," she said. "I was going to a bad place. Natasha helped me help myself. And now that I have cooking in my life, I have purpose. I don't even crave alcohol anymore."

"Well now I feel bad drinking in front of you," Stevie said. "It was right in front of my eyes before, but I never put it together."

"It's okay. I wasn't going to say anything about it. *It* was just going to hit you at some point, like it did tonight."

Stevie looked at his glass of wine, but did not reach over and pick it up.

"Stevie," Madison said. "It's fine. Drink. You don't even drink that much. I want you to feel comfort in knowing that having a drink or two in front of me isn't going to send me down a dark path."

"Are you sure?"

Madison smiled and took Stevie's hand.

"Yes. I stopped drinking because *I* wanted to stop drinking."

Stevie nodded and smiled.

"I don't want to go back to where I was," Madison said before leaning over to give Stevie a kiss. "There are too many good things in my life now to go back to that."

· ·

After dinner, where Jeron went through yet another reenactment of his fumble recovery, Madison dropped him and Natasha off at Natasha's parents' house. Natasha's folks were on another one of their weekend getaways, and the house was clear.

Madison had her own plans for Stevie. Her parents were out of town as well, and Stevie's ankle looked to be just fine.

"Madison," Stevie said from the passenger seat of Madison's car. "You missed the turn. I live off Dandywillow."

"No I didn't," Madison said deviously.

When she pulled into the empty driveway in front

of her house, Stevie knew what time it was. They went inside, and Madison went upstairs to take a shower and "clean the restaurant grime" out of her hair, as she put it. She'd call him upstairs when she was ready.

The anticipation was palpable. The high of a big win was always prolonged and enhanced by that good time with a girl. The main difference was that this time, Stevie actually wanted to be around this girl *after* the deed was done.

"I'm ready!" Madison called from upstairs.

Stevie took the flight of stairs leading up to Madison's room two at a time.

* *

The lights were off in Madison's bedroom. The only beacon of orientation for Stevie was the scented candle lit atop a wooden dresser. She was in bed already, underneath the covers. Stevie could see her wet hair shimmer in the candlelight.

"Strip," she said.

He did not need to hear it twice.

He jumped into bed and underneath the covers.

"You're bouncing around pretty good for someone with a torn-up ankle," she said.

"Motivation."

Unlike Natasha, who oozed sex, Madison was thin and lithe. She had a killer body in her own right. Her breasts were proportional to her frame. Her stomach was flat, and that turned Stevie on too. And finally, her backside had enough padding to be considered womanly.

Madison couldn't keep her hands off Stevie's chiseled frame. It had been a little while for her, and she was ready to get right down to it. Stevie, on the other hand, wanted to take his time and delayed as long as he could. Tiring of the cat-and-mouse game, Madison threw Stevie down on his back, then she leaned down and kissed his neck before moving to his lips. She nibbled on them, and Stevie could smell a faint trace of the garlic they'd had at dinner. He didn't mind.

After they finished, Madison went to wash up. Stevie lay in bed, smiling ear to ear. Oddly, though Madison had been a bit controlling, Stevie wasn't feeling used, but rather that his talents and skills had not yet been utilized to their fullest potential.

11

STEVIE TOOK A MOMENT TO REFLECT. HIS ANKLE felt much better, a testament to the work he'd put in during the past week. The McNeil game itself was another thing altogether. The swinging pendulum of a game left Stevie exhausted, despite not having set foot on the field.

He still wanted to have a heart-to-heart with Jeron about his teammate's drop in play. The night at dinner with Madison and Natasha wasn't the right moment. Though driven and hard to satisfy, Stevie was not an unfeeling maniac when it came to the game of football. He knew how to relax and enjoy a win.

He'd have that talk with Jeron at the right time before it was too late.

Stevie's vision of playing at the University of Texas had been given new life, thanks to his teammates. If the injury before the McNeil game felt like a shocking tragedy, the game itself felt like death from a thousand paper cuts. Stevie had hated the view from the sideline, but the sky was blue once again. He was back. The night spent with Madison was an added bonus, clearing his mind to focus on the task at hand: an undefeated season on the way to a state championship. Deep down, he knew his plan dodged a bullet during the McNeil game. Stevie had to make sure the balance of the season was in his own hands.

The first practice back after the opening game was a decent one for Stevie. Publicly, he labeled his foot at ninety percent; privately, more like seventy-five percent. Nevertheless, Stevie was well enough to practice, and his presence out on the field did not require any lies to Kincaid.

During drills, Stevie's cuts were just okay, though he was not discouraged. He knew his strength and confidence would come back with each passing rep. Robby Steward went back to his spot on the second string. The pangs of competition were no match for the respect he felt toward Stevie.

The team felt like it could win any game under any constraint. As the week progressed, Stevie ramped up his preparation for the second game. Coach Moffit watched his star tailback's reps early in the week, having Stevie alternate with Steward. But by Thursday, Stevie took on the full load, and that was just about the time when his foot felt somewhat normal. The only thing Stevie failed to do in practice that week was cut sharply. He'd save those efforts for the game.

Stevie also made sure to lift the spirits of his young quarterback, Johnny Muretti. The signal-caller's first outing against McNeil was shaky at best. But Muretti did make some big plays that were instinctive and indicative of the kind of player he *could* become. Stevie shared his philosophy about "openness" with Muretti, that when things break down on the football field, the most reliable players are those who have the ability to block out the noise and find "alternate paths." Stevie was one of them. Jeron was too, when his mind was right. The jury was still out on Johnny Muretti.

. . . .

Austin High's second game of the regular season would be played on the road and under the Friday night lights. The game would be against Westlake High School, situated right outside of Austin, only six miles away from Austin High. The cross-town opponent was in the midst of a decade-long down-turn that included no winning seasons.

Though Austin High was heavily favored, that

meant nothing to Stevie. He always felt like the underdog. With preparations for game number two complete, Stevie grappled with the timing for the uncomfortable talk he needed to have with Jeron. To the untrained eye, there was no difference in Jeron's play from the season before, especially from a statistical view. Jeron *was* the same player according to the stats. But stats never told the whole story. Stevie knew football. He knew that if Jeron's missed tackles continued, if the random lapses in concentration persisted, the team would surely lose.

Stevie decided to hold off on the talk for one more week, giving his friend and teammate the benefit of the doubt.

The evening of the second game had arrived, and with it, the belated start of Stevie's senior season. The pain of missing the opening game was matched by the pure, child-like joy of playing in the second one. Stevie could barely contain himself in the visitors' locker room, listening to a playlist of "hype-up" songs on his phone. When it was time for the team leaders to speak up, he pulled out his earbuds and took the floor first.

"I just wanna say I love everyone in here," Stevie said.

The locker room was silent.

"You guys had my back for the first game. And now that I'm healthy, we can go chase this undefeated season. Together," he concluded.

The Westlake game held none of the tension that the McNeil one had. Austin High jumped out against Westlake, with Stevie running for three touchdowns and one hundred seventy-five yards in the first half. This effort sparked Austin to a thirty-five to fourteen lead at halftime.

Even Muretti played a clean game, with Stevie's presence releasing the pressure heaped upon the starting quarterback's shoulders. Muretti finished the game having completed eight of eleven passes for two hundred yards and two TDs. Stevie played only one series after halftime, adding another seventy-five yards plus a touchdown. His final stat line was fifteen carries for two hundred and fifty-six yards and four touchdowns.

Austin defeated Westlake forty-nine to twenty-one, pushing its record to two and zero. The place to nitpick would've been the play of the defense in the first half. True, Austin High was in control with the score at thirty-five to fourteen, but that was due to the offense's proficiency. Jeron's play was once again spotty. He missed a few tackles, easy ones that Stevie had seen him make in his sleep. Jeron had also come up with a few bad reads during the first half, one of them leading directly to an easy Westlake touchdown.

Stevie knew that it was time to have the talk with Jeron. He couldn't afford to keep his mouth shut.

. . . .

After the bus back to school dropped off the players and coaches, Stevie approached Jeron and put a hand on his shoulder.

"Yo," Stevie said.

"What up, player?"

"What are you doing now?"

"Oh, I'm gonna kick it with Natasha. She's on her way now."

"Can you tell her you'll meet up with her later?"

"Why?"

"Let's go grab some food and talk," Stevie said.

"A'ight, why don't you call your girl and the four of us can go to one of those fancy joints?"

"I was thinking just us."

Jeron eyed his friend.

"I'll drop you off at her house after we're done," Stevie said.

"Okay," he said. "Her parents are out of town again. I love it."

"I know you do."

Jeron called Natasha and told her that they would catch up a little later. The two got into Stevie's car and drove over to the Burger Shack. They sat down at a two top with two double cheeseburgers, two fries, a chocolate shake for Jeron and a cherry Coke for Stevie. They ate quietly and ravenously at first, and then Stevie sensed an opening.

"I wanted to talk to you."

"Talk," Jeron said, licking grease from his fingers, and then sipping his shake.

"I've noticed a little difference in your game this season."

"What do you mean?"

There was no easy way to say what needed to be said. In that moment, Stevie wondered if he should even say it at all. But why drag Jeron out to dinner in the first place? No. *This* was important to Stevie. And it *needed* to be said. Stevie was the one who had it on the line. Jeron didn't. His scholarship was set.

Stevie interlaced his fingers and looked down to his half-eaten burger. He closed his eyes and sighed. He looked back up and moved his eyes to Jeron.

He spoke without emotion. "You're missing a lot of tackles this year. You're out of position a lot too. I know you're making some plays. But they're the easy ones. You should be making *all* the plays. You are the most talented defensive player in our section, maybe even the state. But you ain't dominating like you used to."

The bluntness of Stevie's speech took a weight off of his shoulders. At that moment, he wondered why he hadn't always spoken to people in this way when they weren't doing what needed to be done.

Jeron was not receptive. He took a few more sips of his shake while glaring at Stevie. He put the paper cup down. "What are you saying?" Jeron asked.

"I don't think you are trying as hard this season."

"First of all, what do *you* know about playing defense?"

"I know football."

"And second, who are you to question me?"

"It doesn't look like you're giving it your all," Stevie said. "That's what I'm saying."

"Yeah?" Jeron asked.

"Yeah."

Jeron pointed a finger at Stevie. "Let me tell you

something. Not everyone is lucky enough to grow up like you. You got both parents, a nice house. You got a brother who is alive."

Stevie didn't respond.

"My scholarship is the most important thing in my life," Jeron continued. "I lose that and I'm stuck in my situation. And my situation ain't like yours. I ain't got no car dealership comin' to me."

"So you're playing half-assed to not get hurt, is that right?"

"Forget you!" Jeron yelled, "I play my game and you play yours."

Jeron grabbed his shake and left Stevie at the two top.

12

STEVIE'S FRIENDSHIP WITH JERON WOULD NEVER be the same; but he felt he spoke the truth, and because it came from his heart, there were no regrets.

The third game of the season was a Saturday afternoon home affair against Dripping Springs High School. DSHS would pose a defensive challenge because of its strong front seven, which boasted two defensive linemen and two linebackers already committed to Division-I schools. When Stevie saw Dripping Springs on the schedule, he knew he would need to break a lot of tackles in the game.

The game began with a flurry of excitement for

Austin. Stevie broke a long run to the outside on the first play of the game, only to be tripped up at the two. On the ensuing play, Johnny Muretti walked the ball into the end zone on a naked bootleg after a fake to Stevie.

Tragedy then struck on Dripping Spring's first offensive possession. Jeron dropped into coverage on a pass play, and before he had settled into his zone, he took a false step. The irony of his torn Achilles tendon was that there was not another player within five yards of him when it happened. Jeron cried out as he writhed on the turf. The stunned home crowd watched in silence.

Stevie dropped to one knee for his fallen teammate. In that moment of shock, clarity struck and Stevie couldn't help but wonder about Jeron's plan to not get injured before college. Had Jeron sealed his own fate by going half-speed? Stevie shook the thoughts loose and ran onto the field. Jeron was in tears by the time he reached him. He put his hand on Jeron's shoulder but words did not follow. Their eyes were locked as the cart drove Jeron off the field.

Austin High temporarily pushed the grey skies aside by beating Dripping Spring thirty-one to seven. Stevie had another huge game, and another bit of irony occurred with regards to the defense and Jeron's replacement, a junior named Mike Witherspoon. Witherspoon not only filled in for Jeron, but looked like the old Jeron in doing so. He finished the game with ten solo tackles, a sack, and two pass breakups. Witherspoon also played with energy, passion, and clarity. There were no calculations or agendas behind Witherspoon's game. That irony was not lost on Stevie.

Austin's next game would be on the road against Bowie High School, the district winner from the season before. District games were tough for the simple reason that the teams knew one another so well. The contests were also unpredictable. In the season before, Austin had handled Bowie by twenty-one points. Two seasons before, Bowie had beaten Austin by two touchdowns.

On the Thursday before the Bowie High game, Stevie walked into Coach Moffit's office before practice. "Hey coach," he said. "Did UT call about me?"

"No, they haven't, Stevie, but there have been calls on you from D-II schools."

"I don't want to know about those."

Stevie took out his frustrations on Bowie High School, running for three hundred yards and five touchdowns. Austin won the game, forty-one to fourteen, and at four to zero, found itself atop the district rankings.

In three games, Stevie's rushing stats were comparable to many players' season totals. But it still wasn't enough. Not for UT. Not for Stevie. There were more games to dominate, wins to collect, and a state championship to tie it all together. In Stevie's mind, everything was still in play.

A quick turnaround in game number five posed a number of challenges for Austin High. First, the game was on a Thursday night rather than Friday or Saturday. That left less time to heal and recover from the previous game. Second, the game was to be played at Akins High School, another cross-town rival and a team that had made the playoffs the season before.

Stevie's foot was fine, but Coach Moffit decided to give him the entire week off from practice leading up to the Akins game. That proved to be an intelligent decision because Stevie arrived at the game feeling explosive.

Akins' defense had no answer for Stevie. On thirty-five carries, he rushed for two hundred twenty-nine yards and two touchdowns. His night would've been even more impressive if it were not for being tackled at the three before Steward scored on the next play.

Austin won the game twenty-eight to twenty, though the score was not indicative of how the game truly played out. The refs kept Akins High in the game with a bit of home cooking. One major development that boded well for Austin was the fact that Johnny Muretti played his best game up to that date.

No happy feet in the pocket. No passes thrown into double coverage. Just solid quarterback play. That was all the team ever needed.

. . . .

With a full weekend off because of the Thursday night game, Stevie had time to spend with Madison. She was swamped because she'd taken on an extra dinner-shift at the restaurant during the week, but she still met him for dinner and a movie on Friday night after her regular shift. They also spent the night together on Saturday and most of Sunday before their hectic weeks began again.

. . . .

Austin High's next game was at home against Hays High School, from Buda, Texas, fifteen miles south of Austin. Hays's defense bottled Stevie up in the first half by loading the box with nine and even ten defenders. Hays dared Muretti to beat them with his arm—a tactic used by every team that faced Stevie, though few could execute the plan at the level Hays's defense showed in the opening half.

Coach Moffit made an offensive adjustment at halftime to go with four wide-receiver sets in the second half. The thought process was with more room to operate, Stevie could get loose in the second half. It worked as Stevie ran free in the third quarter, amassing one hundred yards and two TDs. Muretti added a touchdown pass at the end of the quarter, and Austin High was up twenty-eight to seven after three. The win over Hays was Austin's sixth of the season, and the perfect start represented the best in school history.

. . . .

Austin had a bye-week next, and with no game to prepare for, Coach Moffit encouraged his players to recover for the late-season push. Stevie rested during this entire time, spending free moments with family and Madison. There was no word from UT, something that saddened Stevie because, historically, colleges contacted coaches over the team's week off. After a brief period of self-pity, Stevie snapped out of it and steeled his resolve. A perfect season was still possible, and he couldn't have been more convinced that an undefeated, championship campaign, coupled with astronomical statistics, would scal his ticket to UT.

The seventh game of Austin's season was a home district game against Lake Travis on a Friday night. The season before, Lake Travis had defeated Austin in a close game in which Stevie had run for one hundred seventy-seven yards and four touchdowns.

After the win, a few of Lake Travis's defensive players were quoted in the *Statesman* as saying that Stevie McCrae was not all that, and in fact, he was nothing special. Stevie took that article clipping and taped it to his bedroom wall, right over his bed, so that it was the last thing he saw at night and the first thing he saw when opening his eyes.

There wouldn't be any words for Lake Travis during the rematch. Stevie did his talking on the field. He ran for a Texas High School state record five hundred ninety-three yards, besting Daryl Ellis's 1998 record by six yards. Stevie also added seven rushing touchdowns and could've gone for the state record of nine had Coach Moffit not pulled him out of the game at the end of the third quarter. Austin defeated Lake Travis fifty-six to ten to push its record to seven and zero.

After rewriting the record book yet again, Stevie thought to himself, *If this doesn't get their attention, I don't know what will.*

13

SURE ENOUGH, THE MONDAY AFTER THE LAKE Travis game, Stevie received a message during first period to meet Coach Moffit in his office at lunch. He walked to the coach's office after fourth period, knocked on the door, and sat down across from him.

"The University of Texas called me yesterday," Moffit said. "It was their lead scout."

"What did he say?"

"He said that your performance in the Lake Travis game was one of the most impressive displays he had ever seen. He also said that the he and the University of Texas were wrong about you."

"Yeah? So does that mean—"

"Well, they want you to walk-on to the team. The school doesn't have any scholarships left to offer for next season. But they said if you're willing to try out as a walk-on, and everything works out, they'll offer you a scholarship when it comes available."

Stevie felt a fist in his stomach.

"Walk-on?"

"That's the best they can offer right now."

Stevie shook his head and stood up.

"We talked about this before. You have quite a few D-II offers on the table. You take one of those, you're the starter from day one. Your college is paid for. And who knows? You light it up, and you can transfer to UT or wherever. Or, you could take the offer to walk-on at UT."

"I'm not a walk-on," Stevie said.

"I know you're not, son. I know you're not."

"What do you think I should do?"

"The same thing I've been telling you. Take one

of the D-II offers. Free college. Starting job. And you go from there. It's a pretty damn good place to start."

Stevie didn't see himself as a Division-II college player. He could not accept that as fact. He felt that if he accepted a Division-II offer, then it would be true.

"No," Stevie said. "By the time we finish this championship run, UT will have a scholarship to offer."

"You really should commit somewhere soon," Moffit said almost pleadingly. "It's late in the process."

"There's time, Coach."

 ·

Just as with the other disappointments in Stevie's athletic life, he let this most recent one slide off his back. One of the things his father had taught him when he started playing sports was not to worry about the things he could not control. Stevie had taken the piece of advice to heart and had become good at applying it to the situations in his life. The only thing he could do at this point was to keep producing: yards, touchdowns, and wins.

Austin won its remaining three district games to finish the regular season with a record of ten and zero. None of the games was close, with Austin's defense finishing the season with back-to-back shut-outs in games nine and ten. The performance of the unit improved after Jeron's season ending injury, something that Stevie secretly predicted. As for his end to the regular season, Stevie took out his latest, personal frustration on those last three opponents, shattering his own regular season totals from the season before.

. . . .

"It looks like you're running from something out there," Jack said to Stevie as the two brothers occupied stools at the wooden bar of *The Dutch Oven*.

"Huh?" Stevie replied.

"When you're out on the field," Jack clarified. "You look like you're running from something."

"What do you mean?"

"I mean, you don't run like anyone else I've ever seen."

"I'll take that as a compliment, I guess."

Stevie turned his attention to the menu. Madison was working that night in the kitchen and told Stevie to stop by because she had convinced the chef to include one of her personal recipes on that night's specials menu. Stevie promised Madison that he'd show up and also thought that it would be a good night for Jack to meet his girl.

"This is it." Stevie smiled and pointed to the list of specials, which was clipped to the restaurant's everyday menu. "The curry goat served over 'Carolina Gold' rice. That's Madison's dish. We both have to order it."

"I don't like goat, fool."

"So what?"

Madison walked through the swinging metal doors wearing her chef's whites. She spotted Stevie at the bar and smiled.

"You made it!" she said on the approach.

Stevie hugged her and put his arm around her waist.

"Madison, I'd like you to meet my brother, Jack."

"Jack," she said.

"Hi Madison," Jack said, putting his hand out for a shake.

Madison did not put her hand out. Jack looked perplexed. "You don't want to shake my hand?"

"I do," Madison said. "It's just that I've been in a kitchen for six hours, and my hands smell like a cross between bacon fat and Madras curry. Stevie's used to it, so I don't mind dirtying him up."

Jack looked at his little brother, and the younger McCrae choked back his laughter.

"I saw your recipe on the menu!" Stevie said. "We're both gonna order it."

"Aw," Madison said with a frown. "Someone just ordered the last two. I'm cleaned out back there."

"Damn," Stevie said. "For real?"

"It's okay—that's a good thing for me! I'll send out some other stuff," she said. "It'll be good."

Madison turned to Jack. "It was nice meeting you, Jack," she said. "I have to get back in the kitchen. Hopefully, we can all hang out after I get off and have that handshake."

Madison kissed Stevie on the top of his head and walked back into the kitchen.

Jack looked at his younger brother and then back-handed his chest.

"She's cool," Jack said.

"Yeah I know."

Jack raised his glass of beer, Stevie, his glass of water.

"To you and your new girlfriend. I wish you two nothing but the best."

"Thanks, Jack."

"And also, here's to you leading your team on a historic playoff run. And to you staying healthy. And to you getting everything you've ever dreamed of out of your football career."

14

High School Sports Section from the Weekend Edition of The Statesman

Playoff Snapshots

District Brackets on A1
Junior Staff Writer: Hal McKinnon
File Photos: Justin De la Cierto

In the bi-district round of the Conference-Six A-District II playoffs, the 10–0 Austin Maroons took on the Cedar Hill Longhorns at a neutral site in Killeen. The Maroons defeated the Longhorns fifty-six to nothing behind the brilliance of senior running back Stevie McCrae. Picking up where he left off during his record-breaking senior season, McCrae finished the game with two hundred twenty-five yards and three scores, including an eighty-yard touchdown run on the game's opening snap. At night's end, Austin High waited to learn whom it would face in the area round of the state playoffs.

. . . .

Playoff Snapshots

District Brackets on A3
Junior Staff Writer: Hal McKinnon
File Photos: Justin De la Cierto

The unblemished Austin High Maroons

faced off with the Dallas Jesuit Rangers in the area round Friday night in Plano. A perennial power from up north, Dallas Jesuit had a down year by its standards and made it to the second round, despite a season filled with devastating injuries. Though at a disadvantage in terms of fan support, Austin High took a fourteen-point lead into the half after three first-half touchdown passes by first-year starter Johnny Muretti. The Rangers keyed onto Stevie McCrae in the first half, holding him to seventy-five yards on fifteen carries. McCrae also lost his first fumble of the season in the second quarter. McCrae, who has yet to sign with a college, turned it around in the second half with one hundred twenty-five yards and two scores. "I'm just on a mission," McCrae said after the game. "It doesn't matter what defenses throw at me. I'm ready for anything." The Maroons beat the Rangers thirty-five to twenty-one to keep their undefeated season alive. The Maroons move on to the regional round, played on the Saturday after Thanksgiving.

Regional Round Opponent Unknown at Time of Print

. . . .

Playoff Snapshots

State Bracket on A1
Junior Staff Writer: Hal McKinnon
File Photos: Justin De la Cierto

The Austin Maroons–who had yet to experience the stain of defeat–squared off against the Spring Hill Panthers in the regional round of the Conference-Six A-District II playoffs at ISD Stadium in Waco. The Panthers boasted one of the best quarterbacks in the country–Kenny Mills–and with him, one of the most potent and sophisticated passing games in all of the state. Early in the second quarter, Austin fell behind seven to nothing on a fifty-five yard touchdown pass from Mills to senior wide receiver Mo Candless. It had been a while since the Maroons had trailed, and the team handled it well, responding with a twelve-play drive, capped off by a seventeen-yard touchdown run from Stevie McCrae. Overall, the first half was a defensive struggle—surprisingly so, due to the potency of the two offenses involved. Looking for a spark, Austin High head coach, Bill Moffit, inserted McCrae to return the third quarter kickoff.

"We needed to get something going," Moffit said. "The game was a slug-fest type of deal. It's not quantum physics or anything like that. When you have a player like Stevie McCrae, you don't have to be a genius to know that the ball needs to be in his hands as much as possible." The stroke from Moffit turned out to be the difference in the game as McCrae returned the kickoff one hundred yards, giving Austin High its first lead of the contest.

The Maroon's defense did the rest, stymieing Kansas State recruit Kenny Mills and the rest of the Panthers' offense on the way to a fourteen to seven victory. On to the next one for Austin, the quarterfinals await against Rockwell High School of Rockwall, Texas.

* *

Playoff Snapshots

Bracket on A1
Junior Staff Writer: Hal McKinnon
File Photos: Justin De la Cierto

The Austin Maroons continued their attempt at perfection in the state quarterfinals Friday night against the Rockwall Yellowjackets. The game was played at Kyle Field in College Station, with the stands split in terms of allegiance. Austin running back Stevie McCrae ran for fifty yards during the Maroons' first possession and capped off the drive with a five-yard touchdown catch, his first of the season. Austin's defense did the rest in the opening half, limiting Rockwall to three first downs and no points. Mike Witherspoon, a junior who's filled in more than admirably at middle linebacker for injured senior, Jeron Peters, shined in the contest, collecting two sacks and forcing a fumble. Austin High defeated Rockwall forty-five to ten and moves on to the semifinals.

*Full Game Report and Analysis in Morning Edition

State Semifinal Commentary + Game-Story

by Senior High School Sports Writer, Wes Gardena
File Photos: Justin De la Cierto

In the first state semi-final, The Austin High Maroons returned to Waco to face the hard-nosed Mansfield High Tigers. On first glance, the game looked to be a mismatch as Austin came in undefeated and had obliterated the majority of the teams on its schedule. Mansfield, on the other hand, started its season slowly, before going on a streak around mid-season and finally catching a few breaks in the playoffs, facing four backup quarterbacks in four playoff games. To the Tigers' credit, they took advantage of the opportunity, riding it all the way to an unexpected semifinals appearance against Austin.

Austin for its part, was confident but not

cocky; when I spoke to head coach Bill Moffit on the morning of the game, he explained that his team had had too much heartbreak in its past to take *any* team for granted. Coach Moffit was already on edge from waking up on game morning at the team hotel in Waco and spotting the potential equalizer right outside his window: a sky covered in a gray sheet, threatening a torrential downpour. Upon laying eyes on this, Coach Moffit knew that any advantages his team had were out the window.

In the first half, neither offense could gain footing on the waterlogged field, and the respective defenses took turns making stops. Given the circumstances, Austin's star tailback, Stevie McCrae, acquitted himself well in the opening half—with one hundred one yards rushing on thirteen carries. However, both promising Austin drives were stifled by Johnny Muretti fumbles during the exchange with center. As Coach Moffit left the field at halftime, he said, "Strategies are thrown out of the window when the weather is *this* bad. The game becomes some kind of vague test of wills that ultimately determines nothing." For what it was worth, before the start of the third quarter, Mansfield's head coach, Roddy Menken, told me that "football is meant to be played under the sun, without precipitation of any kind. But the football gods often have other ideas."

With the score still at a zero-zero stalemate late in the fourth quarter, Austin set out to win the game. Coach Moffit pulled out all the stops to get Austin High to the State Championship for the first time in school history when he yanked Johnny Muretti out of the game and inserted McCrae at quarterback. "Our offensive line hadn't been getting any push the entire game," Coach Moffit said afterward. "My thought process with putting Stevie in at QB was that the ball would be in Stevie's hands from the start of the play and he could choose the best hole–if any–to run through." McCrae gained only six yards on his first two snaps at quarterback. On the third one, he took the shotgun snap, and a hole opened up to his left. He hit the gap hard and fast, and before the Mansfield defense could react, McCrae was sloshing down the left sideline, creating a wake behind him. The fifty-nine-yard touchdown run sent Austin to the state championship game.

The mood in the post-game Austin locker room was one of relief rather than jubilation. I caught up with McCrae outside the team's chartered bus back to Austin. It seemed as though *this* was where it really sunk in.

15

BREAKING AWAY FOR A MOMENT FROM HIS euphoric teammates, Stevie took a seat alone in the back of the bus. He looked out at the rain soaked terrain. He wondered if what he had done was enough. And then he wondered if he was crazy for even pondering the question.

· ·

The state championship game would be held on a late Saturday afternoon in mid-December at NRG Stadium in Houston, where the NFL's Texans played.

There would be no threat of rain because the venue had a retractable roof. Austin's counterpart in the state championship game would be none other than Katy High School, located in southeast Texas, near Houston. Katy was a perennial force, not only in the state of Texas, but also nationwide. The team was ranked number one in Texas and number three in the entire country.

Katy High would travel the short distance to Houston undefeated, but unlike Austin, it did not operate with the rags-to-riches, under-the-radar vibe of a team that somehow stumbled into a perfect season. Make no mistake, Katy *was* Texas high school football, an institution of the highest order. The school from southeast Texas was expected to be undefeated at this point. It was expected to be in Houston in mid-December. And it was expected to win, handily. Everyone expected it.

16

ON THE SUNDAY AFTER THE SEMIFINAL GAME against Mansfield, Stevie was relaxing at home with his family and Madison. His parents, Wilton and Ebony, had met Madison after a home game during the season, and the foursome then went out to dinner near UT's campus. Stevie's folks came away from dinner impressed with Madison's maturity and drive. Although they never verbalized the message to Stevie, he could feel that his parents approved of his relationship.

The family was together in the kitchen, as was their Sunday custom. Stevie's parents were sitting at the kitchen table with Stevie while Madison was teaching Stevie's sister, Naomi, how to properly cook an omelet.

"When you see bubbles on the edges, that's when you flip it," Madison said, with a plastic spatula pointed upward.

Naomi practiced the same technique in a small frying pan of her own.

"Naomi's really taken to Madison," Wilton said.

"She's a sweetheart," Ebony chimed in.

"Yeah," Stevie said.

"So tell me superstar," Wilton said, "what are your big plans?"

"Any advice?" Stevie asked with a wry smile.

"From me?" Wilton asked, jabbing two fingers into his chest. "Nah. You're a man. You can make your own decisions."

"But what about words of wisdom and stuff like that?"

Wilton waved dismissively. "Wisdom's overrated. Besides, with the way you've played this season, you need to make the call. Can't anybody tell you what *your* destiny is."

"I can't believe this walk-on stuff from UT," Stevie said.

Ebony cut her eyes at her son.

Wilton reached over and backhanded Stevie on his shoulder.

"Sorry, Mom."

Madison joined the McCrae family around the table. Naomi had the range to herself now and was planning on surprising the entire family with breakfast.

"I have offers from a bunch of D-II schools," Stevie said before pausing. "Coach also said that he got a call from Rice on me."

"Rice!" Wilton said. "That's D-I. And not far from home."

"I'm thinking that with one more big game, I can get a scholarship at UT," Stevie said. "Probably gotta win the game though."

"Now *that* would be something," Wilton said.

"But Rice, Stevie. That's a Division I school right there, and—"

"It's gonna be hard," Stevie cut him off. "I mean, fighting for *my* spot at UT, but I'll be alright."

. . . .

The Monday before the state championship might as well have been a holiday at Austin High School. The walls inside the hallways were festooned with banners and signs imploring the Maroons to go down to Houston and raise hell. The poor teachers, who already had to contend with the proximity and sway of Christmas, now had to also deal with matters of football supremacy. No student, male or female, was interested in Algebra or Chemistry that week. They could not be bothered with midterms either. It was all about whether the Austin High football team could do the unthinkable and win state.

Stevie tried not to think himself into a frenzy that week. He stuck to his routines, focusing on class work during school hours and football after final bell. He hung out with Madison when both of their schedules permitted. He spent a lot of time around his family as well, the people who grounded him. The season had been a crazy, eventful one, filled with jagged ebbs and flows—from the disappointment of missing the first game to the utter exhaustion of making it as far as they had. Stevie just wanted to enjoy *this* moment. The moment before the actual game. The game itself would be chaos—a physical and mental test that he had yet to experience the likes of. But this time before the bedlam was the sweet part.

17

NRG Stadium was empty three hours before kickoff as Stevie walked along its field by himself. The retractable roof was open, a starless sky in the cards. The entire lower bowl of the stadium and half of the upper bowl were expected to be filled later that afternoon. This was mostly a testament to the easy commute for Katy's loyal fan base. Austin High would have its share of supporters there too, but Maroons' fans were neophytes when it came to cheering on a team at this stage.

Players from both teams began to trickle out of the tunnels and onto the field. Soon, the place was bustling. Stevie watched as fans from both sides swarmed in. When the full-fledged, major league PA system kicked on with Houston's own Bun-B, he knew that this was the real thing.

There was an unexpected visitor on the field about an hour before kickoff. Like the ghost he had become, Jeron appeared seemingly out of thin air and stood behind Stevie as he stretched. Ever since he had had his torn Achilles surgically repaired, Jeron had not returned to class.

Jeron found a break in Stevie's routine and tapped him on the back. Stevie turned and squinted as if laying eyes on a stranger.

"Jeron."

The two shook hands and half-hugged. Stevie looked down to see Jeron's foot in a boot.

"How is it?"

"Still can't put weight on it," Jeron said. "The surgery went well. But they don't know yet."

"How do you feel?"

Jeron shrugged his shoulders and rubbed his hands together.

"I know it would've been hard to be around the team after that," Stevie said.

"It is what it is."

"I'm glad you're here."

The buzz in the air was now beyond hype and palpable. The feeling was something that Stevie wanted to reach out and clutch. Stevie regarded Jeron's face closely, and his former teammate looked like he'd cry.

Stevie tried not to show any of the elation that swelled inside him.

"You know, you were right."

"Aw, man," Stevie said, "I was out of line."

"No, it was true," Jeron said.

"You'll come back even stronger."

"I committed to A&M because they had my back after the injury. UT was trying to pull some stuff, saying that they want to see how my Achilles reacted to the surgery before fully committing to me. I'm going to A&M. This don't begin and end with the University of Texas."

Stevie watched his old friend without saying anything.

"I probably won't be ready till the middle of next season anyway," Jeron said. "I'll most likely redshirt next year. If I can play."

Stevie could see the devastation written on Jeron's face. The thing Jeron had loved had been taken away from him, and the pain of the loss was still formidable. Stevie didn't know what to say.

"You'll play," Stevie said. "You'll play well, Jeron."

"Yeah. Just wanted to wish you luck," Jeron said, putting a hand on Stevie's back.

Stevie nodded, but couldn't speak. They shook hands one last time.

· ·

Katy High School fielded a squad that looked like a professional team. Austin High was no stranger to facing teams larger than itself, but Katy was a different animal in the sense that they were big *and* talented, not to mention fast. These players weren't uncoordinated lugs that took up space. No. These guys could move. And they knew the game, too. Stevie could see that the moment he turned on the game film from Katy's season.

His impressions of the opponent were confirmed while waiting for the coin toss. Katy's captains were all at least double his size. And their stone faces told him that they had been here before and that *this*—the pro stadium, the statewide TV audience, the spectacle—was no big deal.

Katy won the toss and deferred, choosing to throw its defense out there first with the intent to demoralize Austin High from the opening kick. Their mission was to shut down the most potent part of Austin's attack—Stevie.

Stevie walked over to the sidelines and looked up into the expanse of the stadium. The buzz was now a steady hum, a ubiquitous drone. The PA announcer stated that the stands were three-quarters full, but that could've fooled Stevie. It looked like a packed house to him.

Coach Moffit met Stevie on the field and gave him a hug. Stevie wrapped an arm around his coach and closed his eyes. This would be the last enjoyable moment until it was all done. *Whether you win or lose, there is pain involved,* Stevie thought. As always, he was ready and willing to pay that painful price in exchange for being able to perform on that stage.

"They're huge," Stevie said. "Even bigger in person. I hope Johnny has it today. They'll be hard to move up front."

Even Katy's kicker was impressive, booming the opening kickoff through the end zone. Austin's offense took the field, and when it broke the huddle and approached the line of scrimmage, the discrepancy in size between the two teams was startling. As Muretti barked out his cadence, Katy's defensive line shifted. On the snap, each one of Katy's defensive linemen shot his respective gap. Stevie didn't have an opportunity to react after receiving the handoff. He was dumped for a loss of three. On second down, Muretti set up for a quick pass, a simple out-route to the front side to establish a little rhythm and afford a little breathing room. The pass was swatted down by a rangy defensive end. Third and long.

Coach Moffit signaled for a conservative play, a draw to Stevie, because he didn't want anything disastrous to happen to Muretti this early in the game. After taking the handoff, Stevie cleared the charging defensive lineman and was promptly cut down by one of Katy's linebackers. The defender crushed Stevie, placing his face mask right in his ribs. The breath shot out of Stevie's body. It took all he had just to get up. Austin would have to punt.

Katy took over at its own forty. Its offensive line opened gaping holes for its All-State running back to plow through on the first three plays of the drive. By the fourth play, Katy was threatening at Austin's twenty. On the snap, Katy's quarterback, Al Romar, another All-State performer, dropped to back pass.

As soon as Romar saw that his first read was taken away, he took off, just like Austin's defense knew he would.

Coach Moffit bit his lower lip on the sideline. "He's gonna take off, every time."

Romar ran into the end zone untouched. Seven to zero, Katy.

Austin's defense ran off the field, led by Mike Witherspoon. Coach Moffit met Witherspoon at the edge of the field and pulled him close. The stadium echoed with the inescapable chants of Katy's cheering section.

"You know he's gonna pull it down! What did we talk about all week?" Coach Moffit yelled. "After the first read, he's gonna run!"

"I know, Coach!" Witherspoon responded. "He's fast."

"We know that!"

Witherspoon nodded.

"Give yourself enough room to make the play. Just calm down, take the proper angle, and play football,"

Coach Moffit said, with a pat to Witherspoon's helmet.

Austin began at its twenty once again because of another kickoff through the end zone. On first down, the offensive line opened a crease, more than enough room for Stevie to accelerate through and gain twelve yards. Now Austin knew that at the very least, they could get a first down. Two plays later, Stevie took a pitch to the left side. He made the first defender miss, and that created a gap in the defense. Stevie hit the gas down the sideline for a gain of twenty. That play reinforced just how good Katy's defense was. With any other team, Stevie would have been in the end zone after making the first defender miss like that.

With a bit of momentum, and inside Katy territory, Coach Moffit dialed up a shot. Muretti took the snap and dropped seven steps. The protection was there. The QB stepped up into the pocket and launched a bomb to the end zone. Austin's streaking wide receiver, Teddy Fales, had a step on the Katy cornerback, and when he looked up for the ball, it sailed just out of his reach. The Austin sideline gasped at the missed opportunity. The Maroons punted the ball back to Katy two plays later.

At the start of the second quarter, Katy was once again on the move, doing it on the ground, piece by piece, a run of three here and a run of six there. Slow death. By the time Coach Moffit looked up at the scoreboard, Katy had used up almost nine of the twelve minutes in the quarter. And when Katy's running back plunged through Austin's defensive front and into the end zone for the game's second score, the clock read three minutes and ten seconds and fourteen to zero, Katy leading.

Being down two scores, and facing the prospect of Katy's offense after halftime, forced Coach Moffit's hand. He didn't want to play Stevie on special teams, but the time to stay in the game was now.

"Stevie!"

Stevie jogged over to Coach Moffit. "Yeah?"

"Get back there on kickoff!"

Stevie set up in the middle of his end zone. Katy's kicker slipped on the approach, and the kick fluttered. Stevie got on his horse to fetch the wounded duck around his ten. His running start helped set up the return. He burst through the first wave of defenders and juked another in the middle of the field. He found a seam to the right and was off. There was only the kicker to beat now. Stevie figured that he could beat him in a race up the right sideline, and he nearly did. The kicker dove and clipped Stevie's legs from behind. Losing his balance, Stevie stepped on the sideline before tumbling out of bounds. It was first and ten from Katy's twenty, with time to score before the half.

On first down, Stevie took a sweep to the right and gained nine. The clock ran down to a minute and forty-five seconds left. The time to score was now and Coach Moffit wasn't so sure his team could score on Katy's goal line defense. Muretti snapped the ball and faked a dive to Stevie. Austin's offensive lineman blocked Katy's defensive linemen for a split second before letting them rush. Stevie allowed the oncoming defensive lineman to pass, before turning around and showing Muretti his eyes. Muretti just got the pass off to Stevie, an ugly shot put of a thing, before being walloped by Katy's entire defensive line.

Stevie secured the pass and scurried into the end zone behind a wall of blockers. Moffit's call for a middle screen was well timed and the kind of intuitive play call that only good coaches make. Stevie's late fireworks helped Austin High cut Katy's lead to fourteen to seven at the half.

In the locker room, Austin's players looked and felt like they had played an entire game. They had never experienced physicality like this before. Considering the poor start, Austin High's workmanlike approach allowed the Maroons to stay in the game.

Before the second half kick, Coach Moffit reminded his defense yet again to watch Romar's runs. The one strategic change made on defense was to have Witherspoon spy on Romar every time Katy dropped back to pass. That way, if the QB decided to take off, Austin would have its most athletic defender there to give chase.

Katy's first drive of the second half was once again marked by a dominating ground game. The team's offensive line was simply too massive, and Austin's defenders struggled to get off blocks. Coach Moffit knew that his defense would have to overhaul its strategy on the fly against the run, or else the game would be lost. He huddled with his defensive coordinator as Katy set up for a second down play from Austin's twenty-five yard line. On the snap, Romar dropped back to pass, and once again the pass coverage was good, taking away the first option. The QB tucked it to run, and this time, Mike Witherspoon was there waiting for him. Right before Witherspoon closed in to make the tackle, Romar threw a jump pass to a receiver running open in the back of the end zone.

"He's across the line!" Coach Moffit screamed to the ref, who had both arms raised into the air. "Ref! The quarterback was across the line! Come here! Ref!"

Stevie walked over to Coach Moffit as Katy's sideline celebrated the score.

"No, Coach," Stevie said. "He threw it before crossing the line. It was legal."

Coach Moffit ripped off his headset and put his hands on his hips. "Damnit," he said. "Witherspoon played it right, and they still got us."

After the extra point, the score was twenty-one to seven, Katy's lead.

Austin took the ensuing kickoff and quickly drove down the field, mixing in the run and pass, while hurrying up to the line between plays. Austin's tempo and precision knocked Katy's defense off balance. On third and six from Katy's sixteen-yard line, Muretti took the snap and dropped back to pass. Stevie swung into the right flat and was covered by Katy's outside linebacker. Katy's rush flushed Muretti from the pocket, and he escaped to his right. When Stevie saw this, he continued down the right sideline and into the end zone. Muretti lofted a wobbly pass to

Stevie in the back-right corner of the end zone. The ball dropped into Stevie's hands for the touchdown.

The score made it twenty-one to fourteen, and all of a sudden, Austin's fans were the ones in full throat.

Coach Moffit and his defensive coordinator gathered the defense to alert the unit to the change in strategy. Instead of reading the blocks and reacting to them, which were guiding principles for Austin's defenders, the coach charged his defensive line with the task of shooting the gaps on all running plays. This was risky, leaving the defense susceptible to long runs if there were missed tackles, but it was the only way. Austin had to use its speed to create an advantage. The defense had to get a stop.

The tactic worked on the first play of Katy's drive. Austin's right defensive end, Jacobi Newsome, knifed into Katy's backfield and disrupted the timing of the running play. Witherspoon came in and cleaned up the ball carrier for a loss of two. The third quarter ended with the play, as players from both teams raised four fingers into the air.

On the first play of the fourth, Witherspoon used a well-timed blitz up the middle to sack Romar, for a loss of thirteen. It was third and twenty-five for Katy, easily its most difficult situation on offense. Katy called a designed quarterback run on third down, and Witherspoon swallowed up Romar on that play as well. Katy was forced to punt for the first time in the game.

Coach Moffit sent Stevie out for the return.

Stevie fielded the punt and made the first two defenders whiff on their tackle attempts. He broke into the open field and wasn't tackled until the punter tripped him up once again at Katy's twenty-yard line. Livid, Stevie pounded the synthetic turf with his right fist. Getting tackled twice by kickers in the same game were embarrassments of the highest degree. A teammate peeled Stevie off the turf. With a timeout on the field, Stevie ran over to the sideline next to his coach.

"I know what you need to work on this summer," Coach Moffit said.

"What?"

"Getting past the kicker."

With no time to dwell on missed opportunities, Stevie smiled and Coach Moffit followed suit before patting his best player on the back of his helmet.

Austin was in a good position to tie the game. Stevie gained five yards on a first-down run off-tackle. A false start penalty on Austin made it second and ten, and Stevie gained five more on a toss to the left. Coach Moffit knew that Katy's defense would be stacked up against the run on third and five. He looked at his play list and saw a pass that was designed to get the ball out of the quarterback's hands. He relayed the call into Muretti via hand signal.

The primary receiver flashed open on the play, but Muretti held the ball a beat too long and suffered a sack. The play lost six yards, making it fourth and eleven from Katy's twenty-one-yard line. Coach Moffit seethed on the sideline. A sack was the last thing his team needed. The likelihood of gaining eleven yards on fourth down against this defense was low. The more prudent decision would have been to try the field goal from thirty-nine yards out, which was well within the range of Austin's kicker, Keith Tringali.

Coach Moffit sent his kicking team out, and Tringali hit the field goal, trimming Katy's lead to twenty-one to seventeen.

Katy took the ball with the three minutes to go. Austin had all three of its timeouts. In truth, two first downs would seal the victory for Katy. On first down, Katy's running back ran for five yards on first down. Austin called its first timeout. Romar took the ball around the left end for four yards. On second down, timeout number two was called. It was third and one, with the game on the line.

Katy's offense came to the line of scrimmage, and Romar looked over Austin's defense before snapping the ball. He turned and handed it to his running back on a power play to the left. The back burst through the line of scrimmage, broke through an arm tackle, and continued into Austin's secondary.

Refusing to give up on the play, Mike Witherspoon pursued from the opposite side of the field and leveled Katy's running back with enough force to knock the ball loose. Austin's free safety, Myron Sewell, jumped on the ball and squeezed it, as a sea of humanity piled on top of him.

When Sewell stood up with the ball in his hands, the players on Austin's sideline erupted at the same time, all in one action, forming one front. This wave of energy swept the offense onto the field.

There were two minutes and thirty seconds left to go in the state championship. Austin had the ball at Katy's forty-yard line. Coach Moffit called a deep shot to the end zone on first down because he thought that just maybe his team was touched by angels. Muretti's pass was almost picked off.

Coach Moffit nearly jumped out of his shoes as the near interception unfolded before his eyes. He took a deep breath and calmed his nerves because he was not simply a spectator. He had a responsibility to stay calm and call the next play, and Muretti's shaky decision on first down resulted in a predictable play call from Coach Moffit on second down. He signaled in a handoff to Stevie, off-tackle, but Katy's defense snuffed it out based on formation alone. Stevie was tackled for a gain of one. The clock ticked down to a minute fifty as Moffit signaled in the third-down call.

In the huddle, Stevie was in a daze. In his mind, it was all out in front of him, everything—all there for the taking. Muretti snapped the ball, and Stevie swung into the left flat. Muretti hooked the pass out to him. The play that looked like a simple flat pass was anything but. Muretti pivoted and made a half-circle, all the way around to the right flat and then up the right sideline. Stevie faked like he was going to run with the ball toward the left sideline, but then rose up to throw the ball back across the field to Muretti at the last possible moment.

Stevie was clobbered as he released the pass.

Open, Muretti caught the pass in stride and flew down the right sideline. Katy's free safety was the only defender deep enough to make the tackle. Every other player on Katy's defense had done what was preached and practiced all week. They focused on gang-tackling Stevie.

Muretti and the free safety met at the ten, and after the collision, Muretti was down at the five. The clock ran. Though the hit had stunned him good, Muretti had the wherewithal to lift himself off the turf and look over to the sideline for the next play. Coach Moffit considered taking his last timeout to allow his quarterback to get his bearings, but decided to hold onto it. There was still time. No reason to rush now.

Austin broke its half-huddle with a minute to go. Muretti was able to recognize the call: a quick dive to Stevie behind the experienced right side of the offensive line. Stevie almost ran it in for the score on the play, but was stopped just short.

The clock ticked down to forty-five seconds as Coach Moffit sent in the next play. He didn't need to stop the clock now. Katy was out of timeouts. He didn't want to allow Katy's defense to catch its breath. The second down call was a dive up the middle to Stevie. There was no hole, and instead of following his own advice to get low, Stevie stayed high and was knocked back. Third down. Coach Moffit called his last timeout with fifteen seconds left. The offense went to the sideline and the atmosphere in the stadium was surreal. Fans, players, and coaches were silent, as if the wrong words would sway the outcome.

Stevie and Muretti formed a semi-circle around their coach.

"I gotta give you two pass plays," Coach Moffit said to Muretti, scanning over his play sheet. "I don't think there's enough time for a run."

He squinted to see the game clock up on the scoreboard.

"There is if we score!" Stevie said.

"No holes!" Coach Moffit said, still mulling over his plays. "Too risky."

"Let me run it in, Coach," Stevie said.

Coach Moffit looked down at his play sheet again and then at the clock.

"Okay," he said, wincing. "It's gotta be an outside run. They've been blowing our line into the backfield all night."

Stevie nodded. The play call was a pitch to the right. He would have to get to the edge faster than Katy's defenders—some of whom would be already positioned over there, awaiting his arrival.

Austin came to the line of scrimmage for the last time. Johnny Muretti looked out at the Katy defense, prepared to sell out to stop the inside run. He focused on Katy's strong-side linebacker, who was positioned tight to the line of scrimmage.

Muretti snapped the ball and pitched it out to Stevie, going right. Stevie caught the pitch at the five. Instead of getting sucked inside by Austin's misdirection action, Katy's strong-side linebacker made a beeline for Stevie. Stevie had to make a sharp cut—a cut he had made hundreds of times in the past—to avoid the charging linebacker. Although he did manage to elude the tackle, Stevie's balance was thrown. As Stevie tried to regain his balance, a pursuing Katy defender rode him down at the one-yard line.

The clock read all zeroes as Stevie lay face down on the turf.

Katy's sideline erupted with a mix of relief, exhaustion, and utter joy. Their fans rushed the field and joined the players and coaches in celebration. Stevie stayed down for a good two minutes after the final play. A few of his teammates helped him to his feet, and when they tried to lead him into the locker room, he stopped and took a knee in the corner of the end zone he had failed to make it into. Fireworks went off inside the stadium. Coach Moffit sifted through the chaos and confetti and found Stevie. They stood side by side and watched Katy's entire coronation, from the exchanges of sweaty hugs to the presentation of the trophy.

Forty-five minutes afterward, in the church-quiet Austin locker room, Stevie sat at his locker with his game pants still on. All of his teammates had showered, changed, and filed onto the bus to leave the stadium. Stevie's family, along with Madison, entered the locker room and found him there. He stood up to greet them, but didn't do so with words. He hugged his mother and sister first. He then gave Madison a hug, and she smiled sadly, as a way of saying how proud she was of him. Jack put an arm around his little brother's shoulder and tapped his heart with a balled up fist.

"You got a lot of this," Jack said, tapping Stevie's heart repeatedly.

"You played a hell of a game, son," Wilton McCrae said to his son.

"Thanks, Dad," Stevie said quietly.

The family stood silent in the locker room.

"Take some time off after this, son," Wilton said. "Recover. Get your mind right. And you'll decide what you're gonna do for college."

Stevie smiled a somber kind of smile that also revealed a hint of the certainty and optimism that if you looked closely, was really right there, underneath the surface.

"I don't need any time, Dad," Stevie said. "The University of Texas better be ready. They're gonna get the best damn walk-on ever. I'm gonna show up stronger than ever. I'm gonna take that starting running back job. They'll see."